THE ENDLESS SUMMERS OF GOODBYES

William D. Adamson

Cover design by: Art Painter
Library of Congress Control Number: 2018675309
Printed in the United States of America

Thank you to my family and friends for their continued support.

Van, I am so thankful for our conversations. Stay strong.

Ed and Julie, you are still the best.

Love to Lindsey and Julia. Lindsey thanks for your help and thoughts. I hope you like it.

Sydney......Thank you for being you.

And finally to Sarah, "And thy name is like a prayer an angel whispers......."

The Endless Summers of Goodbyes

"You can't live on grilled cheese forever. You're barely 135lbs now!" Kyle said looking down at me with concern clearly in his voice. I was praying at the porcelain altar in our bathroom once again with fresh bandages that covered my lower arms from my latest attempt at ending my life. Sydney had said I have issues finishing anything, I guess she was right. For as many times as I have tried to end my life you would think I would have gotten better at it by now. I looked up at Kyle and tried my best to reassure him that this too might pass in time.

"It's all I can keep down; I need to be able to eat something." It was true, for the last couple of months my body seemed to reject any kind of food apart from grilled cheese. 1996 had not been a kind year so far, now in mid-August, I had just been dealt a terrible blow. The worst thing imaginable, worse than my off and on girlfriend of the last five years dumping me back at the end of May, worse than anything most people could possibly dream up, it was the end of my life. Not being able to eat was a mere bump in the road in comparison to losing what I had lost. I had lost what was most precious to me. It is different for everyone, the one thing that is in each of us that keeps us going in life, that gives us hope and lifts our spirits when things are bad, that gives us the will to carry on.

Maybe for some it is God or a sense of feeling that there is reason for our existence? Maybe it is a place or feeling of belonging to something more? Maybe for others it is the feeling of accomplishment or a measured standard of success? For others though, like me, it is people. People in my life that I find dear and valuable, loved ones that I have grown to count on in times of need or be able to share thoughts and feelings with, and when those loved ones are gone nothing else seems to matter. Only the disparaging thoughts and emotions of being alone. The feelings of emptiness, hollowness, and the inevitable darkness.

I knew my body would eventually allow me to eat. I would not die of self-inflicted starvation. No. My body had already made concessions by not rejecting grilled cheese. I understood why Kyle was worried over my physical condition, but in the end, it has always been my mind that was the biggest threat. The body is easily healed over time, the mind is much harder to fix.

1

"Oh. Hit that real hard!" I yelled to Kyle as I watched my set to him float in the air. Kyle, as if he needed the encouragement, jumped in the air with perfect timing and hit the ball with as much strength as he could muster. The ball, with a nice amount of velocity, hit the sand in front of the opposing team's defender for game point.

"Nice game boys. There are seats next to the court if you want to get in line for a rematch." Kyle said with a little hint of arrogance in his voice. He had learned the art of subtle trash talking from our summer at the beach. I was not as subtle.

"Or maybe practice a bit instead of sitting and waiting?" I added in a mocking tone.

"Screw you both. We'll be back." Jim replied walking off the court flipping us the finger as he did so.

Jim was a friend. A tall somewhat big guy and born and raised on the eastern shore of Maryland. He was a true redneck to the core, complete with an eastern shore accent. A real corn rat. In fact, that had been the nickname that we had given him, and he seemed to appreciate it. Jim had on a few occasions double dated with me back when I had dated Sarah with one of her recently single girlfriends and they had ended with an intimate encounter more than once. Jim, like me, had also lived at the beach this past summer. His job was working on a fishing boat and his dream was to be a true waterman one day. I had no doubt he would reach his goal.

The beach court we played our games on was right in the middle of the common area at the community college we all attended. I had kept my word to my parents by still taking classes, even if it was just part time. The school had built the court and then immediately regretted it and I was one of the few that lobbied to keep it where it was. That sand court was at a great location at the bottom of the common area next to the student hall and the cafeteria with classroom buildings surrounding it as well. The road that circled the campus and lead to different parking lots passed by it too, so basically the beach court was in view of everyone. I rather enjoyed the crowds that would stop and watch if the games seemed competitive enough and by 10am they were usually, with a 3-game wait to play. We only played doubles, and no one ever objected or lobbied for some other game.

"Hey David." I heard a familiar voice yell at me. I looked over to the student hall and noticed a stunning blonde gal with green eyes approaching me.

"Give me a minute Kyle, I better go say hello. No need to piss her off." Kyle grinned and shoved me towards her. She was walking with Dina, another blonde whom I shared a very brief relationship with but now she was always less than friendly when we would see each other.

"Hi Syd." I said then leaned in to kiss the green-eyed beauty. She kept me at arm's length though.

"Uhm no. You're covered in sand." She said a little disgusted with the thought of me potentially getting her dirty. I looked down taking notice of the sand stuck to my body, I was topless and wearing a black pair of Spot Sport shorts and the sand was heavily caked on the parts of my body that were exposed.

Sydney Piccini was a sweet person. She was someone I

cared about, and we had been together for a few months now. She also happened to be the starting setter for the women's college team. She was not very tall, maybe 5'6, but her hands were beautiful when it came to setting a volleyball, and she knew how to run an offense. One of my best friends Kristi had introduced me to her and we just kind of hit it off. It was not like the way it was with Sarah, but it was still good. I didn't not like her; it is simply different.

"Just one little kiss?" I asked giving her the best seductive eyes I could.

"Fine. Just don't touch me with your body. I don't want to be all sandy in my next class." I leaned in and gave her a quick peck on the lips which she reluctantly accepted.

"Shouldn't you be heading to class as well?" Dina added with a little disdain in her voice. Dina is beautiful. She has a perfect athletic type of body, and is a genuinely nice person as well, at least before we dated. Since we stopped, she has not been the friendliest towards me. Dina had not been able to get over the fact that I had eventually chose Sarah over her. Dina and I had dated for about 3 months before I moved to the beach but the problem was I was also dating Sarah. They both knew about each other, but I could never feel anything more with Dina than friendship, no matter how hard I tried. Eventually I ended things with her because she wanted more than I could give, and I knew it was hurting her. I still hoped she could forgive me one day and at least be friends.

"Yeah, I'll head to class in a few minutes." I answered as kindly as I could. The two walked by me heading to their next classes when Sydney turned back to look at me while she kept pace walking backwards.

"Don't forget, you need to pick me up next Thursday for my game. I Love you!" She said blowing me another kiss. I smiled and waved back to her not returning the sentiment.

2

"Dude, did Sydney just say what I thought she did?" Kyle asked me as I made my way back to the court. He was off to the side of the court drinking water from a thermos since he had given up the court to others knowing we needed to get to class. I was watching Sydney and Dina as they were walking away towards their next class, busy in thought about Sydney. She was almost perfect. Almost.

"She started that about a week ago." I answered. I liked the girl, she was a great person, and completely devoted and into me, but love? I was not sure I was there yet and when you are not sure then that really means you are not.

"And?" He asked looking for more information. I knew deep down he was praying Sydney would be the one to help me finally get over Sarah for good.

"And what?" I asked in return hoping he would drop the subject.

"What did you say? Did you say it back?" He pressed. I thought for a moment wondering if I should divulge the information or not. I was not sure how he would take it.

"I said it back, but I feel awful about it and I haven't said it since."

"So, you don't?" He asked looking as if I had just kicked his puppy.

"I don't know, I don't think so." He looked at me in a kind of disappointed way confirming the thoughts I had of his disposition. I knew I needed to reassure him as it had been a tough summer for both him and Weston.

"But I really think I could eventually." I continued trying to get him to understand. "That's why I said it. I don't want this to go down the same road Dina did, and I think there is something there with Syd that wasn't with Dina."

He still looked a little skeptical. Who could blame him? He spent the last 4 months babysitting me at the beach. Well, not entirely. Sydney would come down every weekend and sometimes during the week as well. Kristi would too, and of course Weston had stayed through the summer as he had promised he would. It was not all doom and gloom.

It was a great summer filled with all kinds of adventures. We had learned to surf, played a bunch of volleyball, went golfing as often as we could, and every other beach town activity you can think of. We worked, we played, we lived. We had also made quite a few friends with locals that lived in town year-round and by the end of the summer we had signed a year-round lease. Kyle moved home for the school year but continued to come back every weekend. I stayed but would commute to school and maybe stay the night if I were in the Annapolis area or if it were too late to drive back. Somehow Sydney was ok with this.

"You mean sex?" Kyle said smiling at me. He knew I never slept with Dina, no matter how hard she tried to get me to. I just could not do that while Sarah was still in the picture. I could not do that to either one of them.

"Besides that." I said laughing.

"Alright, I have to get to Calculus. Crabbing later?" He asked me. We loved crabbing. The act of catching them is a lot of fun, picking the meat out not so much. They do taste amazing though and it is a fun way to pass a few hours in between or after classes.

"Maybe, I want to head home early tonight. I have to work

tomorrow."

He said his goodbyes and I watched him head up the hill. He stopped momentarily to hug a familiar person that I had not expected to see. I watched as they chatted for a few moments then hugged again as they parted ways. Kyle heading off to class, and Sarah heading straight for me.

3

I was not prepared for this. I had not seen her in over six months and although my mental state had improved drastically, I was not entirely sure I could handle seeing her. I could not run as that would be a little obvious that I did not want to talk to her, and the truth was that I really did.

Walking towards me her long blonde hair was floating in the wind just off her shoulders. Her blue eyes staring at the ground as if maybe she was a little unsure of if this was a good idea to talk to me as well. She was wearing a light blue denim shirt that was unbuttoned and tied in a knot at her waist over a white tank top. Light Blue Jeans that were the exact same color as her shirt with a brown braided belt and brown flats. She looked amazing, like she always does, as she had a talent for looking her best no matter the clothes she was wearing or the style of her hair.

As she got closer, I decided to make myself look busy by putting my stuff into my backpack. She stopped a couple of feet away from me and watched for a moment as if gauging what my reaction might be to seeing her.

"Hi David," she said in a gentle but unsure voice. Good I thought to myself. She is as nervous as I am. I looked up from what I was doing squinting my eyes a little as I was looking into the sun.

"Hey Sarah. How are you?" I answered back in an un-interested voice.

"Fine, I guess. Can we talk?" OOhh. There's the trigger word 'Fine'. I knew that meant she was not.

"I was just getting ready to head out. I have to get back to the beach." I was not but I decided at that moment it was time to leave. I was not ready for this and I could feel that I could crack inside if I continued this interaction. My heart was racing, and I knew if I spoke too much I would sound like a bumbling idiot.

"I'm leaving too. Can we talk on the way to our cars?" She asked determined to talk. What could she have to say that was so important? Reluctantly I nodded my agreement and we started walking towards the parking lot.

4

We walked in silence for the first 10 minutes toward the lot. You could cut the tension with a knife. I could not tell what kind of tension it was though. Was it the kind like when I kept forgetting to get her number for the first 3 times we talked or hung out 3 years ago, or was it the kind of tension I felt right before jumping in front of that moving car just 5 months ago? I could not tell, but I was leaning towards the latter.

The fact that we were walking together had not gone unnoticed by others that I wish had not seen us together. I smiled and waved to three different gals that played on Sydney's team that were met with casual waves, and stares back. I would hear about this later, I was sure. A short little brunette ran up to us at full speed stopping just two feet in front of us. She was all smiles and could not contain her obvious enthusiasm about who I was walking with.

"Hey David!" Kristi said in an overly exaggerated voice acting as if she had not noticed Sarah. Kristi had quickly become one of my truest and best friends over the last 9 months. A cute tiny little thing at barely 5'2, but if you ask her, she is 5'3 and a half. The thing with Kristi though is that we are simply great friends. There was no real attraction whatsoever. I loved her though in a sisterly kind of way. She reminded me of Cathy in a way and a couple of girls I had dated after Sarah would call her for advice if we were having issues. So, without ever meeting her she knew all about Sarah from Dina and I am sure Sydney as well.

"Kristi, this is"

"Sarah." She finished the introduction for me before I could and gave her a one-armed hug.

"It's nice to finally meet you. I've heard a lot about you." Kristi said looking at her. I slapped her shoulder hard enough to make her flinch.

"Ow, sorry. I didn't mean anything by that just that it's nice to meet the girl the others constantly cry to me about." I slapped her shoulder again.

"Ow stop!" This made Sarah smile a bit.

"I think it's time you go. I'll call you later or stop by on my way home." I said staring at her.

"Ok. Ok." She turned to look at Sarah. "It was nice meeting you. I wasn't trying to be mean. Really." I grabbed Sarah by the elbow and ushered her away. Of course, she turned around to talk to Kristi as I was escorting her along.

"Nice to meet you! Let's talk sometime!" Sarah yelled to Kristi.

"No, you won't." I said only loud enough for Sarah to hear and not looking back at Kristi.

"Yes! Let's get together sometime!" Kristi yelled back. When Sarah stopped fighting the direction we were walking in, I let go of her arm.

"She seems nice." Sarah said kickstarting the conversation.

"This isn't an "enjoy the silence" moment?" I asked still not looking over at her. She did however look over at me though. She was trying to gauge my feelings I kind of thought. Trying to determine if this would be a productive conversation or not.

"No, I told you I wanted to talk." I could not resist her any longer, I gave in and looked up into her eyes, and then I smiled.

"She's the best. I'm so glad I met her. She's like Kyle, or Weston to me. One of my best friends. Someone I can always count on." Sarah turned to face forward again not understanding that Kristi and I were just friends.

"It's not like that at all Sarah. She truly is just a friend, one of my best friends, yes, but that's it."

"Ok" she said nonchalantly as if still not understanding.

We had managed to make it to her car, and she was leaning up against it. I could tell she wanted to say something but could not find the right words. I figured I would help her out.

"So, what's on your mind Sarah?" She stared at me for a long time and then shifted her gaze to the ground unable to handle my looking back at her. The only thought in my mind was please do not cry Sarah. I could never handle seeing her cry.

"I just wanted to know how you were. That's all."

How am I? I had not given that much thought lately. I mean I was better than I was, but did that mean I was actually good? I was quasi whole again but pieced back together with Scotch Tape. I decided to answer honestly.

"I'm fine" Haha. Take that I thought. She nodded her head in response. She knew. She always did. I could never slip anything by her.

"Fuck you David! You still suck!" Jim yelled from the other side of the lot. We both looked over at him.

"I love you too corn rat." I yelled back. Sarah laughed a little.

"Hi Sarah." He said waving as he got into his Ford Bronco that smelled of feet and dead ducks on the inside of it and then sped away through the parking lot.

"You still have a way with people." She said still smiling.

"I guess." After a few hard awkward moments, she decided to speak again.

"Well if you can't open up to me then how about something a little easier? Like, I don't know, tell me about the beach." I smiled at this.

"I love it! I can't imagine being anywhere else right now."

"What took you there?" I thought about how to answer this for a bit. I could not tell her it was an escape. She did not need to know that. To my knowledge she was still in the dark about my attempted suicides and there was no need to disclose that to her now.

"You know you've met Kristi before, right?" She looked puzzled by the question and perceived change of subject.

"I have? I don't remember that."

"Well, it was a brief introduction. Remember when I was dating Dina, but it was your Saturday with me? Kristi had that party that my volleyball friends were all going to and Dina insisted I needed to go even though she knew you'd be there too? We walked in and you saw Dina and proceeded to kiss me as long and hard as you could. She then ran outside crying and threw up." Sarah put her head into her hands embarrassed by the retelling of the incident.

"Yeah, I made us leave right after that, but not before introducing you to Kristi."

"I kind of remember that night. I'm fairly sure I had been drinking before we got there."

"Well, I ended things with her later that week, but of course you still weren't ready to be exclusive again so Kristi and I would hang out. We would drive out to the beach on Friday evenings and then come back later that night."

"You guys would come back the same night?"

"Yeah. We'd spend maybe three hours there then drive back. Anyways, I kind of decided along the way I wanted to live there. When you and I quit talking, I made the move. Kyle and Weston went with me for the summer, but then Kyle and I signed a yearlong lease, so he comes up on weekends and I commute to school twice a week."

She thought about this for a while trying to digest it all. "Wow. And your current girlfriend doesn't mind you being so far away?" She asked. How does she know these things? I had not mentioned Sydney to her. I had not had the chance to yet.

"Sydney? I'm not sure. We've only been together since June. She comes up a lot and I come back a lot. She hasn't said anything about it yet."

"Do you love her?" She stared into my eyes and right into my soul. I did not answer.

"Well?" She was not going to let me out of this.

"That's so unfair. You know how I feel. Why make me voice it to you? You know I'll never feel the same with anyone else the way I feel about you." Shit! I did not catch that in time.

"Felt. Felt about you." I tried to correct. "I like her though. She's a lot like you." Sarah nodded.

"Good. I'm happy for you. I really am." A tear rolled down her face. I lost all control at seeing this. I dropped my backpack, reached out and grabbed her, and pulled her into a hug that she eagerly returned. She cried softly into my shoulder and with every tear my arms tighten just a bit. I wanted to hug the tears away from her. I was not entirely sure why she was crying; wasn't it Sarah that had ended things between us? Wasn't it her that wanted us to be free and date others? She stopped contacting me, right?

"Sarah, why are you so upset? Wasn't this what you wanted?"

She pulled away from me instantly and wiping her eyes as she did so. Sarah opened her car and started to get in and then looked back at me. I could still see pain in her eyes.

"You're still an idiot." She said and got in her car slamming her door closed.

"What did you want to talk about?" I tried to say in a loud enough voice for her to hear. She put on her sunglasses and sped off out of the parking lot without saying another word.

5

I stood in the parking lot a few minutes longer and waited to see if Sarah would come back. She did not so I decided to head to my favorite little spot on the water and wait for Kyle to show up for some crabbing. I made the 10-minute drive to the pier that is off the Severn River and thought about my conversation with Sarah. I did not understand why she was so upset, and then to flip on me like that as if I had done something wrong? I was baffled. Am I as big of an idiot as she thinks I am? What was I missing?

"I was hoping you would be here." A voice said interrupting my thoughts. I looked up to see Kyle standing there.

"Sydney was wondering where you went. She seemed a little pissed." Kyle said walking up to me. I was surprised to see him not carrying the crabbing stuff. He sat down next to me on the bench facing the water.

"Is she now?" I asked in a somewhat condescending voice.

"Her exact words were "Where the fuck is David?" This have anything to do with Sarah?"

"I would assume so. Like three of her teammates saw me walking with Sarah. I'm sure Sydney knows by now."

"And?" He asked wanting the details.

"And what?" I said looking over at him. He gave me a suspicious look.

"Nothing happened. She said she wanted to talk so we talked, but then she left mad for some reason." He turned back to the water.

"You're an idiot." He said shaking his head as if I somehow disappointed him.

"Why does everyone keep saying that?" I asked perplexed by the situation.

"You need to figure that out on your own. I can't tell you that." He answered as if by telling me why I am an idiot it might ruin the journey of discovery. I stood up from the bench and started heading for my car.

"You are leaving?" Kyle yelled to me as he watched me make my way to the car.

"Yeah, I need to get back and I have a stop to make before I do."

"Tell Kristi I said hello." He yelled back to me.

6

Kristi lived in Cape St. Claire right off the Bay. I loved her parents' place. It was a home away from home to me sometimes. Her parents were wonderful people that were accepting of my dropping in unannounced from time to time and allowed me to crash there if it got too late for the drive back to OC. I always slept on the couch, but even if I had crashed on the floor in Kristi's room, I always had the feeling it would have been ok with them since they knew nothing was going on between us.

I rang the doorbell and was told by her father to go on up to her room. As soon as I got to the top of the stairs, I could hear her talking to someone. I assumed over the phone as I heard no voices in response, just a one-sided conversation.

"No Sydney, I haven't heard from him yet since seeing him at school" she said as I walked into her room. She looked up and put her finger over her lips signaling me to stay quiet.

"If I see him, I'll tell him to call you." She said into the phone. I sat on her bed next to her but faced her. I could not hear what Sydney was saying but I could tell from Kristi's facial expressions it was not a conversation she wanted to be having.

"Yeah, I saw him with Sarah." She said into the phone and then gave me the finger.

"I don't know, I didn't ask him what he was doing with her." This time she punched my shoulder.

"Look Syd, I need to go. I'll call you later, Ok?"

"Alright I will, bye" She said then hung up the phone.

"Sorry?" I said looking as apologetic as I could.

"You're an asshole! Why would you get caught hugging Sarah?"

"I didn't know anyone saw that." I said in my defense.

"Half the team saw you together, you didn't think at least one would follow you and observe and report?"

"You volleyball chicks are ruthless. I thought you guys all secretly hated each other?"

She smiled at this. "We do. I'm sure they all told Sydney, not to be good friends, but knew it would start trouble and piss her off."

"Oh my God that's awful, but true I think." I agreed. She took my hand in hers and got a serious look on her face.

"David, for my birthday I know what you can get me."

"Your birthday isn't until December, but what is it?" I asked her curious to what I could give her.

"Just two weeks in a row where your women don't call me wanting information about you. That's it. Just two weeks free from whiny bitches."

I laughed at this. "How am I supposed to accomplish this?"

"I don't know." She said sighing. "You might as well tell me about what happened with Sarah though."

"Fine. I'll tell you on the way to the beach though. Get your stuff and come with me."

7

The drive to the beach was spent recapping the whole day. I left out no detail. I told Kristi about Sydney's expressing her love, volleyball, and of course my conversation with Sarah that still had me perplexed. Kristi would stop me every now and then to ask a question here and there but for the most part just listened with her head leaning on her hand. She seemed rather amused by the whole thing. She liked Sydney well enough, she liked the girls on the team too, but I always felt she somehow managed to stay above all the drama. I think it is one of the reasons I liked her so much. She managed to stay above it whereas I managed to be the center of it no matter how hard I tried not to be.

"So, tell me, what's the deal with Sydney? And Sarah?" She asked looking over at me as we crossed over the Rte. 50 bridge into downtown Ocean City.

"Sydney is great. She seems into me, like really into me." I answered looking over at her. She stared at me hard.

"That was not much of an answer." She said almost scolding me for the lack of feelings I expressed.

"I don't know. I like her?" I said sounding like more of a question than a statement. Her stare remained.

"So, she's convenient." Her voice said the thought disgusted her a bit.

"That's a little harsh." I said to her in response.

"You still love Sarah, don't you? Jesus it's Dina all over again." She turned her gaze out her window watching the sun reflect off the hotel windows that lined Coastal Highway.

"I probably always will." I admitted knowing the truth of the matter.

"Then you should never have started anything with Sydney."

"You introduced me to her! Oh meet my friend Sydney, she's a really good volleyball player, you have so much in common, she's so pretty." I said imitating her voice.

"Yeah. Yeah. Yeah" She said in response waving her hands as if to tell her something she did not already know.

"It's not that I don't like her, I do. I'm just not in love with her. Yet." I felt I needed to say more so I continued. "It may happen. I'm not looking to dump her or anything like that."

"That's romantic" Kristi said looking at me in disbelief. She continued to look at me as if searching for something I was not telling her.

"Why Sarah?"

"What do you mean why Sarah?" I said pulling into Pizza Tugos to grab us some dinner for when we got back to my house. I ordered a large pepperoni pizza which to me was like eating a little slice of heaven. It smelled divine and I could not wait to get home and devour it completely. There were never any leftovers when we ordered Pizza Tugos.

"I mean why Sarah? Why do you keep going back to her? It's like she looks at you and you crumble."

"True." I said agreeing with her assessment.

I thought about it for a moment, and thankfully Kristi was willing to give me that time in order to answer the question. She had returned to staring at me though and it was not the most comfortable of stares. It was the kind of stare that expected no bullshit and nothing but the truth. I have never held anything back from Kristi, in fact I had always confessed everything to her, I shared real feelings with her like the way I was able to with Sarah. Kristi may have been the next best thing to Sarah but in a purely platonic way.

"Sarah is like home to me, or at least how I think home should be. Like coming here, or when I go back to Ohio, I don't know, comfortable, like a warm blanket. I feel safe with her and wrapped in love. Even if we aren't "together". I don't know how to describe it."

She continued the stare. "You're so screwed." She finally turned her gaze out to the front of the car and then added "And so is Sydney."

8

I pulled into the driveway out front of my place. A little two-bedroom place on Jamestown less than 3 blocks from where I had spent my beach week at Jeremiah's. It was great this time of year as there were not many of us that lived in town during the offseason, but the weekends were still quite lively. I had not noticed the red Nissan parked in the other spot designated for our house and when Kristi and I got out of the car she grabbed the pizza while I grabbed her overnight bag. When we made our way up to the front door, I noticed someone sitting on the front steps leading up to the door.

"Hi David." Sydney said then looked over at Kristi, "Kristi" she added with a little hint of anger in her voice.

"Oh good! You two can talk. I'm going in to eat." Kristi said without skipping a beat. Either she missed the fact that Sydney was upset at us being together or she chose to ignore it knowing she and I are harmless together I did not know which, but I loved how she dismissed the attitude either way.

She took the keys from my hand and opened the door, leaving me alone with Sydney. I stepped closer to give her a proper greeting when she put her hands up blocking me from the attempt.

"Did she tell you I was looking for you and wanted you to call me?" She asked me still clearly angry over the current situation.

"Hi Sydney. Yes, she did, but I wanted to get back earlier rather than later and planned on calling you when I got here." I said trying to remain calm, it was not working though. I could feel myself going into defensive mode, which would eventually turn into offensive mode if I were not careful.

She folded her arms across her chest. I could tell she was pissed. The thought occurred to me that she did just drive two plus hours to basically have me hear her out face to face. In a way it was kind of a turn on. I mean, no one does that unless they care right?

She looked good considering the drive and the fact that she had spent time before driving here looking for me. She was wearing black leggings and a red sweatshirt where the neck had been ripped off so it hung down to her shoulders. Her long blonde hair was naturally on the curly side and would curl even more when it was humid outside, and her eyes may have been the greenest eyes I had ever seen. They were even prettier when they had fire in them like now. I could not help but smile at her.

"Don't do that." She said pointing her finger at me apparently still angry.

"Do what?" I asked back still smiling.

"Smile at me when you know I'm mad. It irks me." I stepped closer to her and this time she let me. I put my arms around her and embraced her in a hug which she did not return.

"And why are you mad at me? What did I do this time?" I said into her shoulder. I could smell her skin and it reminded me of lavender. I loved the way she smelled as it always made me think of flowers whenever she was close to me.

"You know damn well what you did, and why is she here?" She said motioning with her head behind her towards the house where Kristi was currently inside eating our pizza.

"You're upset with what the peasant girls told you. About seeing me with Sarah. And Kristi is here because she's my friend and will always be welcome here. She's here because I invited her."

"So, you tell me. Since you feel, it was inaccurately portrayed to me."

Shit! Why won't she just accept that it was nothing? I ended my attempts at hugging her since she still had not embraced me back but kept her defensive posture.

"Sarah asked if she could talk to me. She seemed upset so I agreed, I walked her to her car and that was it."

"And you needed to hug your ex why?" She asked with a little more anger in her voice.

I hated the peasants even more now. The ones that just start trouble to see the others suffer to make themselves feel better about their own lives.

"Her grandfather is sick and may not recover. She told me because I've met him and really liked him. I hugged her because we were friends once and a friend needed the hug. That's it. No more." That was the first time I lied in order to save Sydney's feelings and in defense of Sarah. My mood changed though, and I went on the attack. "And as far as Kristi goes, get over it. She and I are close friends, nothing more. You can either accept it or leave now, but I will not stand for you giving her grief or being jealous of her. Am I clear on that?" She waited a moment digesting all that I said and then embraced me hard.

"I can accept your friendship with Kristi. I like her too and I know she has been there for you during some really tough times. I just wish you would have that kind of connection with me. I guess in a way I am jealous of her." She withdrew from the embrace and the fire returned to her eyes.

"Sarah though, I can't handle that. I won't accept the idea of her being in our lives. I can't be in a relationship with you feeling like I'm in her shadow. Either let her go or let me go."

I stared back at her gauging her resolve. I thought I had let her go. It was one conversation that I felt had said nothing but apparently everyone else thought had said everything. I reached for her hand and took it in mine, then leaned over and kissed her.

"I know Sydney, I know." I opened the door behind her and held it open inviting her in. "Now let's go eat before Kristi finishes off that pizza." She smiled at me as she walked through the door never realizing I agreed to nothing.

9

The evening had been pleasant enough. To my surprise Sydney did not make the evening as awkward as she could have. Instead, she was friendly and polite to Kristi, even though I knew she still harbored some slight jealousy towards her. She did her best to bury those feelings and at least act appropriately. As I said, she is a genuinely nice person.

The three of us had passed the evening away eating pizza and playing Family Feud on my 3DO gaming system. It was fun, and as the night got later Sydney and I had gone up the stairs to my room to go to sleep for the evening. I could not sleep though. Unsure of the reason why and feeling the need to talk to Kristi I decided to head back downstairs. When I got halfway down the stairs, I leaned over the railing to see if Kristi was still awake. I could hear the TV was on, so I thought that was a good sign. As I made my way down the stairs I could see she was laying on her side with her eyes closed so I decided to go back to my room and try and sleep since it seemed she was sleeping.

"Did you screw her?" Kristi said in a tired voice. I turned around and went back down the stairs and took a seat in the chair opposite the couch she was laying on.

"What?" I asked not understanding the purpose of the question she had asked.

"You heard me; did you screw her?" I thought about the question, did I really need to answer this? Was it any of her business? I had not, but I was a little unclear as to why it mattered to her.

"No. I didn't." I finally answered. She sighed, a little in

relief I thought.

"Good. Why are you down here?" Her voice was tired, and she seemed slightly annoyed at my presence.

"Why are you happy about that? It's not like it wasn't offered." I replied.

"David, It's late. What do you need?" She was getting more and more aggravated with every passing moment.

"I just wanted to talk."

"About Sarah?" She asked me. I nodded slowly the confirmation. She sat up and pulled her long dark hair behind her shoulders then motioned me to come sit next to her. When I took the seat next to her, she gave me a friendly hug and lowered her voice. I assumed to not wake up Sydney. I could tell her aggravation of my interrupting her sleep had disappeared.

"That's why it's good you didn't sleep with Sydney." When she pulled away, she saw the quizzical look on my face.

"You don't need to talk; you need to listen." She stated in a more serious tone. I nodded again so she knew I understood to allow her to talk uninterrupted.

"I never should have set you and Sydney up. It's obvious you are still in love with Sarah." She rubbed her arms trying to chase the cool air in the room away.

"Want me to start a fire?" I asked her seeing how cold she was. She nodded and I set about the task of building a fire in the fireplace. One of my favorite things about this place was the fireplace, second only to the view of the bay. I would make fires all summer long no matter how warm it was. It was a calming influence to watch the flames dance as the wood would burn.

"David, you need closure with Sarah, one way or the other. You need to talk to her. Find out what she wanted to talk to you about. If there's even a chance you two can be together you need to find out and take it. Before Sydney falls too hard for you."

"It's because I love her that I had to let her go!" I said in my defense raising my voice above the hushed tones she was currently using.

"No girl wants to be let go! And you didn't even tell her that, you just stopped talking to her entirely. Without giving her a reason."

"She wanted the break! She wanted us to be free to date others. I never wanted that!"

"Who could blame her? You told me about it, you were kind of a douche to her. You got off easy. If that were me, I would've slapped you around a bit and then maybe chopped some things off you. Trust me, she did not want it to end the way it did. With months of silence from you."

I thought about her opinion as the fire crackled behind me. She was right of course. There had never been any sort of closure. The thought though of talking to Sarah scared me. As if reading my mind Kristi stood up and hugged me again.

"I know you're scared. I know you were hurt, but if you don't do this, you'll spend the rest of your life wondering what if." I hugged her back. She really was an amazing friend. It seemed like sound wisdom that she was passing on to me.

"You're right. I'm scared."

"Don't be. You're not the douche you used to be." That made me laugh.

"You're stronger now."

"What about Sydney? I do like her you know." I asked.

"I know, but not enough. Yet. It can never be anything though until you talk with Sarah. I'd wait to say anything to Syd. You may not need to say anything at all."

"You are almost as bad as I am." I said to her while exiting the hug.

"Almost." She said smiling up at me. "You do make for good entertainment David Anderson."

10

It was almost 4am and the fire had almost burned all the way out. The room was no longer cold, and we were both still on the couch. I was sitting up with my feet propped up on the coffee table while Kristi was half laying on me and half on the couch at the same time. We both had our eyes closed, half asleep, half still talking.

"What if she says no?" I asked groggily. It felt like minutes would pass between our responses to each other.

"What if she says yes?" She finally replied. She snored slightly for just a brief moment then woke back up. I smiled hearing her answer.

"I'm not sure I want to end things with Syd." Another long sleepy pause.

"You loved Sarah enough to let her go. Like Sydney enough to not hurt her more than it already will." My smile left at that reply. That was a horrific thought to me. The knowledge that Sydney would be hurt. She was so perfect, and her only downfall was us being together while Sarah and I were still so connected.

"Is there a way to have both?" I asked Kristi. Not out of selfishness, but out of the fear of hurting Sydney. Kristi sat up abruptly coming full awake.

"Are you fucking serious?" She said in an angry tone. "This isn't that tramp in Dundalk you told me about and Dina. It's Sarah, whom you love, and Syd whom you think you could eventually love under the right conditions."

"Jen was her name, and what's your point?"

"You actually have feelings for these two, where you didn't with Jen and Dina. Sydney is a friend, and I think Sarah could be, someone is already going to be hurt, possibly all 3 of you, at least with Dina and the whore there weren't real feelings there. Pride was the only thing hurt in that situation."

"OK, I see your point." I replied not liking her opinion but knowing the truth of it.

"Talk to her, then decide what is best." She said laying back down.

The stairs creaked from the weight of someone walking down them. We both knew who it had to be, and Kristi sprang up into a sitting position. No need to make Sydney anymore jealous than she had to be. Sydney turned on the light to the stairwell revealing herself. She looked like she just woke up with sleep still in her eyes and her blonde hair pulled back into a ponytail. She was wearing my robe covering the silk blue nighty she had worn to sleep in.

"Are you coming back to bed David." She asked me. I could tell she was a little annoyed, but mostly only tired. I stood up and made my way to the stairs as my answer. Sydney turned and went back up to my room seeing that I was coming as well.

"Hey." Kristi said in a loud whisper. I turned to look at her waiting for her to finish her thought.

"Don't you screw her." She said smiling at me. I smiled back and wished her goodnight.

11

The next day was full of all sorts of fun stuff. It started with Sydney leaving early as she had to get back to class. Since it was a Wednesday, I did not have to make the drive back and Kristi decided she could stay as well and not hitch a ride back with Syd. The day was warm, and we did the typical beach thing, wanting to soak up the sun and feel the sand.

We packed a cooler full of Bud Lights and made our way out to the beach to bask in the sun. To make it easy on us we only crossed Coastal Highway to the other side and parked up near the entrance to the beach rather than heading downtown to a busier street. Laying on towels we had brought we were content to feel the warmth and drink the beers. We had not really talked about anything serious since the night before and I knew it was eating her up. I honestly think that is why she stayed the extra day because the thought of spending two hours in a car with Syd without talking to me first seemed daunting to her. That thought made me smile.

"I didn't sleep with her." I said breaking the ice and letting her know it was ok to talk about it.

"Good boy." Kristi replied with sincerity. I cracked open another beer and handed it to her.

"What number is this?" She asked.

"Your fourth."

"What time is it?" She asked with a little hint of concern on her face. She might be feeling the drinks I thought. I checked my watch.

"2pm."

She took a drink from the beer. "No more after this one for a bit. I want to enjoy the day and not be plastered. How was she this morning when you guys woke up?"

"Fine. I think." Sydney had seemed ok to me, but I have been told lately that I am an idiot so I could have misread how she was really feeling. "Maybe a little quiet. I figured it was the idea of driving back though that she was dreading."

She laughed at me "You are an idiot David. You think that brief conversation you had with her where you tried to explain your interaction with Sarah was reassuring enough to her?" She laughed some more "Get real."

We stayed for another hour and then packed up and went back to my house. When we walked through the door, the phone was ringing, and she ran to answer it for me. I think she secretly likes causing trouble. She knew if it were Sydney, it would irritate her a little that she had answered my phone. Especially since Sydney never would think to do that. Sydney viewed my stuff as mine. She was only a guest at my place and had no right to anything there, even answering the phone from her perspective would be overreaching her privileges of being my girlfriend.

"Hello?" Kristi asked with a smile on her face. Her eyes scrunched up a bit listening to the other person.

"No this is David's place; you called the right number." Her face brightened a bit as if recognition must have set in as to who it was.

"Yeah, he's here. Can I tell him who's calling?" She started silently laughing hysterically as the other person answered.

"Oh Hi, this is Kristi." She said to whomever was on the phone.

"Yeah, I came down for a couple of days."

"Let me go grab him for you. You should come down

tonight. It would be fun. The three of us could hangout and we could tell stories." She said still laughing to herself. I made my way to her and the phone wondering who was possibly coming. She saw me and quickly ducked into the other room wanting more time with the person on the other end. I reached for the phone willing to take it by force if I needed to.

"Ok. Here he is, I got to go. Bye!" She got in as I wrenched the phone from her. She took a seat at the kitchen table and looked up at me.

"Oh, this day just got interesting." She said to me. Now I was curious. I pressed the phone up to my chest so the other person could not hear me.

"Is it Syd?" I asked Kristi confused why Sydney would get such a reaction out of her. Plus, she talks to Sydney all the time, she would recognize her voice, so why all the theatrics?

"No" she said shaking her head still pleased with herself. "Even better." Comprehension started to set in. Could it be her?

Kristi stood up then yelled "Bye Sarah!" loud enough as to make sure Sarah would hear her on the other end of the line. I closed my eyes while still pressing the phone to my chest. I can do this I thought to myself. I took a deep breath and then spoke into the phone.

"Sarah?" I asked just to make sure Kristi was not kidding. Although if she were, and it was Sydney, that probably would not have been the right thing to say either.

"Hi David, yeah it's me."

Thank God I thought to myself.

"Hey there. How are you?" The thought occurred to me that I had not given her this number. How did she get it? Previously, before we were together, she had called my girlfriend at the time for it. For some reason Barbie had given it to her. Probably because Barbie never viewed Sarah as a threat. I could not imagine Sydney doing that as Sydney had all but admitted she is worried about Sarah.

"You didn't call my girlfriend for my number, did you?" It came out more as an accusation than a question.

She laughed though at the question. "No. I called Kyle and he gave it to me and I'm fine. Thanks for asking." There's that word again. "Fine". I knew now she was not.

"Are you ok to drive?" I asked her.

"Yes. Why?"

"Because whatever you want to talk about, I don't think it should be done over the phone. We owe each other that much at least."

"You want me to come to you?" She asked a little skeptical of the thought.

"Or I could drive to you." I offered back. One of the other phones in the house picked up.

"No, he can't. He's been drinking. You need to come here Sarah."

"Get off the phone Kristi!" I said yelling up to her. Sarah laughed at the two of us.

"Uhm, I guess I could come up." She said still a little reluctant.

"Sarah, you don't have to if you don't want to."

"But he really wants you too!" Kristi said into the phone.

"Oh my God I'm going to kill her!" I said to Sarah.

Sarah laughed again.

"She's right though, I'd like it if you came to hang out. We can talk when you're ready, but I can at least promise you dinner first." I said trying to sweeten the deal. She thought for a long moment in silence.

"Please? I'm so bored here by myself." Kristi said into

the phone acting as if Sarah would be saving her from her current unbearable situation of being a hostage here with me at the beach rather than being here willingly.

"Uhg, OK. I'll come, but I expect to be fed!" Sarah finally said.

"I can do that." I assured her.

"And we talk when I'm ready and not a moment before. I'll tell you when."

"He can do that too!" Kristi said into the phone. I rolled my eyes. I may kill her yet.

"OK then. I'll see you soon." Sarah said and then hung up the phone leaving Kristi and I alone on the line.

"I told you this day just got interesting." Kristi said then hung up as well leaving me the only one still on the line.

12

"Trust me! She'll love it if you cooked that." Kristi said voicing her opinion on what I should make for dinner. She had gone grocery shopping while I took a shower to clean up. I thought we had agreed on the menu. Apparently, I was wrong.

"I was really looking forward to spaghetti." I said pouting a little as I did so.

"No girl drives for two hours for spaghetti, don't' you know anything?" She said with a disgusted look on her face that said she thought I was stupid.

"Yeah, but shrimp stuffed with Crab Imperial? And wine? Don't you think that's a little much for the three of us?" I asked. She looked at me and shook her head.

"You really are an idiot. Now get cooking."

I set about to the task of cooking this grand meal for my close friend and my ex-girlfriend. It still seemed a little much to me. Kristi had poured us each a glass of wine when the front door opened. I was shocked to see Kyle walk in. He usually only comes down on Friday evenings and stays through Sunday, so seeing him on a Wednesday was a little shocking. He sniffed the air taking in the aroma of what was cooking.

"Damn that smells good!" He said excited to be eating soon.

"It's almost ready, maybe another ten minutes or so." I said back. "What are you doing here anyway?" I asked him. He looked over at Kristi and then I saw Sarah walk through the door. Now I'm even more confused. Kristi stepped to Kyle and took his arm.

"I called him. I was worried about Sarah driving down by herself this time of night." Kristi said feigning concern.

"It's not even 6" I reminded her. She waved her hand as if what I said was of no concern.

"Whatever." She handed Sarah a glass of wine and refilled my glass.

"Yeah, Kristi called me, I called Sarah, then I called Kristi and figured since you two needed to talk, it was probably best if she and I went out for the evening and gave you two some space." Kyle said wrapping his arm around Kristi.

I looked at both. They had sly smiles on their faces. I looked at Sarah and could tell by her expression she had nothing to do with this and now seemed a little uneasy about the two of us being alone at my place, at the beach, eating a nice dinner, and drinking wine. That and she kind of was stuck since she rode with Kyle. Kristi patted Kyle on the stomach and left her hand there.

"Let's go big guy. Take me to dinner."

"Sounds good. What are you in the mood for?" They started walking to the door as the oven timer went off. Kristi looked back over her shoulder to me.

"Spaghetti sounds good. David went a little overboard with the dinner he's making." I threw the oven mitt at her as hard as I could nearly hitting her in the head.

"We'll be back by 8" Kyle said as they walked out the door. I looked at Sarah who was now staring at me.

"You've got to believe me, I had nothing to do with this. It was all them." I motioned over to the stove with the baking dish on it. "Even this, Kristi bought for me to make us all I thought." She smiled at the thought of that. She walked over to me and rolled up her sleeves.

"It smells good. What can I do to help? Hi by the way." I smiled at her.

"It's Shrimp stuffed with Crab Imperial with broccoli and rice. Help me set the table?" I asked.

She went right for the cabinet containing the dishes as if she knew exactly where they were. I went back to completing the dinner I was making. The kitchen was small, and we tried to stay out of each other's way without much luck. Occasionally bumping into each other and casually smiling to one another when we would. At one point she reached over me to get the silverware from the drawer in front of me and it was then that I noticed her. I mean really noticed her.

I could smell her shampoo, and the soap she uses that was oh so familiar. She was wearing my white Maui and Sons sweat-shirt that had somehow become hers a couple of years ago with blue jeans and her black flats. Her hair had been pulled up into a ponytail.

"You look nice." I said to her not sure why I felt the need to compliment her, but she smiled back at me appreciating the compliment.

To make it easy on us, we brought the plates from the table and we served ourselves from the kitchen and then went back to the table to eat. I held up my glass to make a toast which she followed the gesture.

"To sneaky friends." I said. We touched our glasses and she smiled while repeating the toast. We ate for a few minutes in silence, and I was eager to get to what she had rode in a car with Kyle all this way to say.

"So, Sarah," I began. She shook her head at me.

"Not yet. You agreed to let me talk when I was ready and not before. Can we just enjoy dinner first? It's really good. Thank you for cooking." She said cutting me off mid thought. She was right though, it was good, and I had agreed to letting her tell me her thoughts in her own time.

"I was just going to ask you how the drive was." She stopped chewing the bite she had taken and look at me half closing one eye. She knew. She always knew when I was not being totally honest.

"No, you weren't." I laughed a little at her response. "The ride was fine. Kyle and I talked the whole time. Time just flew by. I miss talking to him."

I studied her for a while watching her eat and trying to solve the mystery that apparently made me look so stupid to everyone. She put her fork down only halfway through the food I had put on her plate. She stood up, refilled our glasses of wine, and grabbed my hand ushering me away from the table.

"Let's go out on the back porch. If you can't let me eat, then let's try relaxing."

We went out to the back porch that faces the bay. I lit the tiki torches as to have some light and grabbed a couple of throw blankets in case she got cold. We each took one of the lounge chairs that were reclined all the way back into laid down positions and turned to face each other. I did not say anything waiting for her to speak first. I knew she was nervous as she raised her eyebrows and made her eyes get big a few times as if asking me "what do you want? Quit staring at me." Finally she began to speak. At long last I would know what apparently, I was not smart enough to figure out before.

"David, I need to know, why did you just stop talking to me? I loved you and I feel like you just quit on us. I always thought you would learn to love life on your own and then we would be back together, so why did you just quit loving me?"

Her words hurt me to my core. How could she see it that way? Wasn't it her that wanted us to date others? Wasn't she the one that quit calling me? Didn't she tell me repeatedly that she was not ready to be back together? I thought about these things for a long time, could I have been blinded by my own feelings? Was I only seeing what happened from my point of view? She still looked into my eyes waiting for an answer. I could not lie to her; she would know right away.

"Sarah, I never stopped loving you."

"So why did you stop talking to me."

Neither of us were angry. This was not a fight, but merely a calm quiet discussion. She was trying to figure things out, maybe get closure even.

"I never wanted us to date other people" I said to her in a somewhat accusatory tone shifting the focus to what she wanted back then rather than what I had wanted.

"Neither did I." She stated flatly. "Then again, I never hooked up with other guys while we were together, I never did destructive things to myself or others, I wasn't out stealing and vandalizing things in the middle of the night, and I certainly didn't ignore you for weeks because I was pissed off at you either." She looked up at the night sky trying to hide the tears forming in her eyes.

"Just saying." She added as if trying to lighten the mood.

She was right of course. I had admitted as much the night I tried to kill myself in the bathroom. I had freed her that night. I knew it was all me so why couldn't I admit that to her now? Was I trying to protect myself from her? She never hurt me, it was always a result of my own actions, so why am I back to blaming her? She had no blame in the way things happened.

"You're right. I'm sorry." She looked back over at me as if to see if I believed that or was just trying to make her feel better.

"Why did you just quit? I need to know." She asked still holding back tears.

"Sarah, I thought I tried everything to make you happy. I sent flowers, I sent cards, I tried to spend as much time as I could with you, I tried to do the things you wanted. I lived my life for you!"

"But you didn't listen." She said raising her eyebrows to make her statement somehow more meaningful. I frowned not understanding.

"I didn't ask for those things. I asked you to figure out what makes you happy besides me. One person can't be responsible for another's happiness. We could be happy together, but I can't be the sole reason for it. I wanted you to take that time and find it yourself." I laid there still looking at her and remained silent. "And look." She said holding her arms out wide as if demonstrating something. "You did. You found whatever you needed here at the beach."

She was right. I had been happy here. I felt like life mattered outside of Sarah again. I nodded to her my understanding.

"But then you had to go and get a new girlfriend! Why?"

I sighed before answering her. "I thought you'd be happier without me."

"Who told you that? That was the worst thought ever."

"No one. I decided that on my own. I guess I needed to lose you entirely in order to find what I needed to. I had to accept you not being in my life." She stood up and came over to my lounge chair and motioned for me to scoot over. Once I had she laid down next to me and wrapped my arms around her so I was holding her. It felt good, it felt natural, it felt right. I kissed the top of her head.

"I never did. I could never accept you not being in my life." I did not answer her, but I did squeeze her tighter. We laid there for a while in silence. I noticed her breathing had changed and I realized she had fallen asleep. I felt a single tear fall from her eye and land on my hand. My heart ached once again for Sarah Fulton.

13

I was startled awake by the sound of what sounded like a body flopping to the ground followed by another. I could hear muffled laughter from inside the house as recognition set in, Kyle and Kristi were home and whatever they were up to was loud. It sounded like they were having fun, but way too late for a Wednesday night in the middle of September for the amount of noise they were making. I tried to sit up and pull my arms away from Sarah without waking her without success.

"What's wrong?" She asked with a tired voice. Her eyes squinched closed and frown lines appeared on her forehead. She was never one to be aroused from her sleep unwillingly and to be cheery about it.

"Sorry. Kyle and Kristi are back and are making a lot of noise." She lowered herself back down into my arms. I could feel her shiver as the night had turned cool. Another loud crash and possibly the refrigerator door slamming? Now Sarah was curious as well as she sat back up. Muffled yelling and more laughter came from inside the house as I looked over at Sarah. The sleepiness had apparently left her, and she seemed a little more ok with being awake.

"Want to go see what they're up to?" I asked her.

"Sure. Sounds like fun whatever they are doing." I stood up and then helped Sarah up by taking her hands and pulling her upright. I opened the sliding glass door for her, and we made our way to the kitchen where all the noise was emanating from.

"Don't you do it! Don't you dare throw another egg!" Kyle's voice rang out. Kristi laughed and right as we got to the entrance, I saw an egg fly by and break against the wall.

"Now you're going to get it little one!" Kyle said in a raised voice. Sarah and I walked into the kitchen towards the sounds of all the commotion.

"Oh my God! What are you two doing?" I asked angrily taking in the scene.

There were raw eggs, that had been apparently thrown, broken all over the walls, Peanut Butter smeared on the floor and countertops, leftover Chinese hung from the cabinets, pizza stuck to the stove, and all sorts of other foods and condiments that had been apparently thrown or squirted seemed to cover everything. The kitchen looked as if a tornado had only hit the refrigerator, emptied it out, and deposited the contents all over the kitchen.

Kyle and Kristi looked just as bad. Kyle was covered in eggs and what I assumed was pancake batter, Kristi did not look any better with Peanut Butter and Jelly smeared all over her face and body. Kristi still held an egg in each hand, and Kyle held raw hamburger meat in his. Obviously, it was a food fight that had gone on way too long.

Sarah came to stand next to me and started to giggle upon seeing the scene as Kyle and Kristi both stopped their respective assaults on each other and looked over at me. They must have been home for a while as it was well past midnight, and both had changed into sweats and tank tops. If I were not so mad about the wasted food and the mess, I would have found this amusing. They looked cute all covered in food.

"He started it." Kristi said motioning over at Kyle with her hand still clutching the eggs.

"True, but she wouldn't let it end! She just kept grabbing more stuff out of the fridge." Kyle said pointing back at her.

"Oh, so this my fault?" She asked then let the egg fly pelting him in the chest. The egg hit with enough force to shatter sending raw egg everywhere. Sarah and I instinctively ducked as to not get hit.

Kyle charged over to her and pushed his hand holding the raw meat over her head smashing it into her hair and down her face. They both slipped on the floor slick with vegetable oil and landed with Kyle slightly on top off Kristi. Both were laughing hysterically. Then the unthinkable happened, he kissed her. She seemed to not only accept his kiss but return it in earnest and then crack the remaining egg over his head mid kiss.

They did not stop kissing though, even as the egg dripped off his head and down onto her cheeks, they just kept kissing as if the only thing that mattered was each other. Sarah leaned up against me and I could not help but think how it reminded me of my prom after being pushed into a lake by Sarah and then carrying her into the water as well. At that time, the only thing that seemed to matter was each other. Not the being wet, not being cold, not that we were still with Weston and his date, but just each other. I wondered if Sarah was thinking about the same thing.

"OK, knock it off you two. I'm still standing here." I said a little too angrily. When did this attraction between the two of them happen? Why not tell me? They stopped kissing and the laughter ensued again from them. Kyle sat up allowing Kristi to sit up as well.

"Let's go get cleaned up before he loses his shit." She said to Kyle. They stood up and she took his hand in his as they made their way up the stairs.

"Separately!" I yelled to them. They stopped and looked over the railing to me. "And guess who's cleaning all this shit up? And buying all the groceries?" I said still a little too heatedly.

"Ok dad." Kristi said as they continued up the stairs and out of sight giggling the whole way.

14

I was pacing back and forth. Ten minutes had passed. Ten minutes! Still no Kyle or Kristi yet.

"What are they doing?" I asked to no one in particular. I could hear giggling every now and then though coming from upstairs.

"They're having fun. Why are you upset by this?" Sarah answered watching me as I paced back and forth.

"Come sit with me." She said motioning to the spot next to her on the couch. I looked over at her as she held out her hand beckoning me to come sit with her. I made my way to her and gave her my hand and then sat next to her turning towards her to face her.

"Seriously. Why are you upset? Aren't you happy for them?" I thought about her question. Why was I mad? I should be happy for Kyle and Kristi, not angry with them.

"Because. They didn't tell me." The whine in my voice made me think of my dad.

"Maybe it just sort of happened?" She said making it sound like a question. I looked into her blue eyes. Her eyes, filled with kindness, immediately softened my heart.

"Maybe?" I sighed a little sigh. "I guess I'm ok with it."

"You're jealous!" She exclaimed looking shocked at the same time. I looked away from her. "You are! You've had this great friend that you didn't have to share and now you're afraid of losing that to Kyle." She always knew exactly what I am feeling.

"Yeah, I guess that's it." I said a little reluctantly.

"Don't be worried. They both still love you. They will both be great friends for years to come." Sarah has this serious look on her face and I am not sure what came over me, was it our previous conversation? Or the wine earlier? Or the way she looked at me in that moment trying to ease my angst, but I leaned in and kissed her. Slow at first, and then, as if she decided to accept what was happening, it turned very hard and passionate, and she eagerly returned the kiss.

"Well, well, well. It seems somebody is in a better mood!" Kristi's voice echoed from the stairwell. She was followed closely by Kyle. Both were cleaned up and both looked wet from a shower. I wondered if they showered separately or together? The thought of them showering together irritated me. Kristi was sporting Kyle's robe and a towel wrapped over her head. Kyle wore some mesh athletic shorts and a sweatshirt. I stared at them both feeling displeasure rise in me.

"Or maybe not?" Kristi said stopping short of the couch standing near the fireplace. She looked over at Sarah as if pleading silently for help. Sarah must have picked up on the silent cue as she wrapped my arm around her and snuggled up close to me purposely rubbing her body up against mine just enough to get my attention.

"Babe do you know if I left my blue Quiet Storm sweatshirt at your house? I can't find it." Kyle said not paying attention or noticing the atmosphere he was walking in to.

He stopped next to Kristi noticing her looking at me, then me looking at them, and finally Sarah trying to distract me and attempting to keep me calm.

"Oh boy." He said sheepishly stepping behind Kristi who had taken on a defensive posture folding her arms across her chest. Sarah gripped my hand tighter.

"At her house?" I asked. The thought disgusted me. Had

he been to her house? Without me?

"Shhh. Be still." Sarah whispered to me.

I relaxed a little remembering what she said about both being lifelong friends. Then, looking at Kristi and knowing she was prepared to set me straight, I smiled. The smile gave into laughing which caused Kristi to start laughing. She then ran over and plopped herself on my lap hugging me.

"Sorry Sarah." She said knowing she pushed her out of the way. Kyle still looked a little perplexed as if not entirely understanding what was going on.

"I'm happy for you both. Just tell me how long this has been going on for?" I asked Kristi. She looked over at Kyle.

"How long Babe? Two months?"

"12 weeks, not quite 3 months." Kyle corrected.

"He's so sweet. He remembers everything." She said smiling at him. Kristi stood back up and dashed over to Kyle kissing him on the cheek.

"Why didn't you tell me?" I asked them still a little dumbfounded. They looked at each other as if seeing who would answer. Kyle took the initiative.

"We wanted to, but we weren't sure how. And we wanted to make sure you were ok first." Sarah frowned not fully understanding that part.

"I was going to tell you sooner, but every single time other drama happened." Kristi added. I could see that. Most of the time she and I hang out is when things are not exactly perfect with me.

"I was going to tell you earlier, other things happened. I'm sorry we didn't tell you sooner." She added. As if once again on cue Sarah tighten her grip on my arm.

"Shh. Be Still." She said quietly to me. I looked down at her, kissed her quickly, and knew everything would be great.

"I'm the one who's sorry. For reacting that way. I'm happy for you both. Let's build a fire and enjoy the rest of the evening."

Kyle set to the task of the fire while Kristi poured more wine for everyone. When all had their glasses, I proposed a toast.

"To sneaky friends." I said clinking the other glasses.

"Sneaky friends" The three of them repeated.

15

The evening passed telling stories. Mostly experiences that Kyle and I had over the summer. Some of which were a surprise to Kristi. A few interesting ones about Weston, but mainly it was catching Sarah up on the last 6 months that she had not been around for. It was a little odd seeing my two sneaky friends sitting close to each other and holding hands, but as the night went on, I got more and more use to it. The night grew late, and everyone decided to get some sleep. Sarah and I watched as Kristi followed Kyle up to his room.

"Best part about David knowing now is not having to sleep on that couch anymore!" I could hear her say as she followed behind him. I shook my head in disbelief. Sarah laughed as the bedroom door slammed closed and more giggling ensued from the bedroom.

I looked at Sarah still looking to the stairs. "How did I miss that for the last 3 months?" I asked her.

"Were you looking for it? Maybe your thoughts were elsewhere and so you missed it?"

"True. I've been a little self-centered lately." Everyone had told me to focus on myself though. Get right in the mind they said. "But still, I was never able to hide how I felt about you from them when we first got together. Even now they plotted to get us together. I must not be as good at hiding my feelings as I thought." I added.

Sarah smiled. "No. You aren't."

I looked down at my Swatch watch checking the time. It was almost 3am and we all needed to leave no later than 7am to make it to our first class.

"Sarah, you can sleep in my room. I'll take the couch."

"I'm not kicking you out of your own room. I'll take the couch. Is it as bad as she said it is?" She asked looking over at the couch not at all sure she wanted to sleep there. I stood up and walked over to her extending my hand to her. She looked at my hand and then to my eyes but eventually she placed her hand in mine. I pulled her up, then led her to the stairs and without hesitation she followed.

When we climbed into bed, we were both fully clothed. I had laid on my side propped up on my left elbow, so I was able to look at her. She was laying on her back looking up at me. Again, we kissed.

"I won't sleep with you." She said to me breaking the kiss.

"I'm not asking you to."

She rolled over onto her side pushing her body up against mine. "But I'll let you hold me if you'd like." I laid completely down so I could wrap both arms around her. It seemed we had once again melted into each other.

"This though, this feels right." She stated as if memories were flooding back into her mind. She smiled a small smile. "But no more while you have that girlfriend of yours. Goodnight David." She added closing her eyes and looking completely relaxed.

Her words haunted me. "That girlfriend of yours." I had forgotten all about Sydney. What would I do about Sydney?

16

The next couple of days flew by, and I was no closer to figuring things out in my personal life than I was earlier in the week. I was stuck in an emotional vise with no idea what to do. My only refuge, living two hours away at the beach, was no longer the safe haven it used to be. Kyle had come for the weekend, as he usually did, but this time Kristi had accompanied him. Sydney was here as well. I was used to her being here on the weekends, but this weekend was different. She insisted on coming where normally I must invite her. I did not mind, but after this last week and all that happened with Sarah, it felt somewhat wrong for her to be here. What could I do? Sydney was worried about us, and rightfully so I guess, but she did not have all the information. With what she knew she really had no reason to be concerned. If she knew the rest, she absolutely would have the right to be worried.

I really do like Syd, I could see us together for a long time, but I loved Sarah. If only Sarah had said we would be together, but she never said that. She said she would like to see where things would go. I would be giving up my sure thing with Sydney for a chance with Sarah. Why couldn't Sarah just be all in with me? It would make this decision so much easier. I understood why she could not or would not, I had hurt her badly in the past, and like me, she was protecting herself.

The real kicker though is everyone knows how well I have handled loneliness up until now, and it was not pretty. The thought of ending things with Syd and then Sarah not committing to me was a lonely thought. Sitting there on my couch, deep in my thoughts, I had not heard Kristi and Kyle come in through the front door. They had been checking out little flea markets a few miles inland in Delaware for most of the day.

"And these are the Days of Our Lives" Kristi said to me seeing I was alone in my thoughts.

I jumped a little as I was surprised to hear her speak. Kyle made his way to the kitchen dropping bags of groceries onto the counters. Days of Our Lives is a soap opera Kristi liked. I preferred All My Children and One Life to Live myself, but I got her little jab. I looked up at her and saw she was holding an umbrella holder that looked like a red rooster.

"That's cute." I said pointing to the rooster. "Your parents going to like it?" I asked. It was a little on the ugly side I thought.

"It's not for my parents, It's for you guys." She said beaming. I looked over at Kyle who had cracked open a beer. He was giving me a look that said, "Just go with it." Obviously to me he was not excited about the rooster either. I looked back over at Kristi who was putting the ugly rooster next to the front door.

"But it's ugly." I said coldly. Kyle, hearing my words, snorted beer out of his nose. "And we don't own any umbrellas" I added trying to make the first comment less harsh.

Kristi waved me off as if my opinion did not matter. "Nonsense. It has character. It's perfect. What do you think hon?" She said looking over at Kyle expecting him to agree with her opinion.

He looked at me and saw the expression on my face. He knew it was hideous and I was hoping he would sack up and say so. He looked back over to her and put on his overly charming, extremely irritating to me, smile of his "You're right babe. It looks much better there than in the store."

"Oh my God. You are such a liar. There is no way that thing looked any uglier in the store than it does here." I said rolling my head away from him.

Kristi took the seat next to me on the couch. "How are

you?" She asked changing the subject. I could hear the empathy in her voice and see the concern in her eyes. I ran my hands through my hair out of frustration.

"I have no idea what I'm going to do."

She patted my hand a few times in understanding. "You'll figure it out." She scanned the room as if looking for something or someone. "Where's Sydney? You didn't sleep with her, did you?" Her voice expressing the concern she had over the issue.

"She's upstairs cleaning the bathroom. Apparently, it isn't up to human standards, and no, I haven't had sex with her."

Kyle looked surprised at this. "You haven't? I thought you guys had? Like all the time." He asked confused.

"Not in the last week. Not since I've been talking to Sarah again" I said clarifying for him. As if on cue Sydney came down the stairs. Her hair was up in a high ponytail and she was wearing one of my older IE T-shirts and sweatpants. Full on in cleaning mode attire. When she got down the stairs, she noticed the rooster and smiled.

"Hey guys! Love the umbrella holder!" She said smiling to the three of us. I laid my head back on the back of the couch. Kyle took another drink from his beer but chose to stay quiet. Kristi smiled.

"I think it adds character." Sydney added.

"I thought so too." Kristi said standing up and walking over to Kyle embracing him in a side hug.

"It's growing on me. Thanks for getting it for us babe." He said kissing the top of her head.

I stood up from the couch realizing I had lost this battle. The rooster was going to stay. I knew there was no way of making it disappear now. "I'm going surfing. You coming Benedict Arnold?" I said looking over to Kyle. He looked down at Kristi still hugging him from the side as if asking her permission.

"It's fine with me." Kristi said. Sydney, full of energy, bounced over to me flopping on the couch. "Can I go too? I wouldn't mind sitting on the beach and relaxing while you two surf." She asked me looking up with her green eyes.

She really was a beautiful thing. A little prissier than Sarah, but a similar personality. Very kindhearted. I really did not want her to go though as I needed to sort through my thoughts.

"Why don't you come too babe? You could hang out on the beach as well. Maybe find some of those shells you were talking about making a necklace out of?" Kyle said looking down again at Kristi. Kristi looked over at me as if getting my approval. She knew I wanted to escape and not have a group outing. I knew this too was another battle I would not win if I tried so I gave her the slight nod as if saying "you might as well come too." I could tell she understood.

"Uhm sure. I'd like that." Kristi said. What she really meant was "thanks Kyle for trapping me on the beach all by myself with Sydney so I'll have to hear her complain about David for the next hour plus".

I looked back at Sydney who was still waiting for me to answer her. "Sure. Let's get going though. I want to hurry up and get there while the surf is still up. I heard it's almost chest high."

She stood up, still smiling, and leaned up and kissed me thankful for my approval of them tagging along. "I'll get changed and be ready in five minutes." She said bounding up the stairs like a gazelle being chased by a lion. When she had disappeared upstairs, I looked over at Kyle and gave him the finger.

17

As the weekend went by my situation only seemed to get worse. I was no closer to figuring things out. As Kristi had said, this was not Jen or Dina, this was Sarah and Sydney. One from the past who I always prayed would be in the future as well, and the other in my present. I never expected the future to get here so quickly.

My confusion on what to do was starting to show as well. If there is one thing I had learned long ago, it is that if my interest was fading for a girl, I was not good at hiding the fact. Of course, Sydney picked up on this. Bless her heart though, the girl was as patient as any saint ever was. By Thursday evening, I knew in my heart that she absolutely loved me.

The week had gone as normal as it could, I guess. I would talk to Sydney as often as I could on the phone and would talk to her at school on Tuesday. I also did the same with Sarah. My conversations with Sarah were happy and upbeat whereas with Sydney they were cold and somewhat sullen. I would see Sydney early in the day on Tuesday at school, then later in the day hang out with Sarah. Deep down I was praying the peasants would catch me with Sarah so I would be spared any kind of conversation with Sydney. If that is what I ended up deciding. Thursday though, that was as self-destructive as I had been in a long time. I knew I had to pick Sydney up by 2:30 to take her to her game, but things came up.

"Hi, you have time to walk me to my car?" Sarah asked me. I was cleaning myself off from the last game of volleyball when she walked over to me. I checked my watch quickly and noticed it was only 12:30. I had time.

"Hi there. Yeah, sure thing. Let's go." I answered her back.

We made our way through the common area of the campus to the lot where we had both parked. We had recently worked out where we would park to be as close as possible in the last couple of weeks in order to be able to walk each other out. When Sydney had asked me why I switched lots, I gave an excuse about being closer to the gym so I could shower after playing if I liked. The lies I told to cover up for Sarah and my "relationship" were starting to mount up. As usual, Kristi was walking towards us smiling her little smile that said "I know the secret, I know the secret" in a child's mocking tone.

"Hey David. Hey Sarah." She said giving us both quick hugs. Then she waved to a couple of the peasants from the team walking nearby. I gave her a look that asked what are you doing.

"Relax. They already saw you." She said to me. She was right of course. I was prepared to hear about this later. Kristi looked at Sarah. "When are you coming back to the beach?"

Sarah looked over at me and saw me staring at Kristi with my mouth slightly ajar in disbelief. "Uhm, I don't know. Whenever he invites me, I guess." She answered shyly and a little embarrassed.

"I'm inviting you." Kristi replied matter of fact like. "Screw him." She said nodding her head over at me. Sarah laughed and once again I found myself forcefully ushering her away from Kristi without saying goodbye to her.

"Don't forget to be at Catonsville by 4:00!" Kristi yelled to me as I forced the brisk pace to our cars. I let her go and slowed our pace when I was sure Kristi would not attempt to follow.

We walked in silence all the way to her car, a light metallic blueish Toyota Tercel, which was parked next to my car. Once we got there, we turned to face each other. I had not noticed in our brief glances and smiles at each other, but she looked a little sad to me.

"So." She started but then paused as if waiting for me to say something. I raised my eyebrows trying to get her to continue. "I'm guessing you still have that girlfriend."

The thought occurred to me that this must have been how she felt. Can we talk about something else? Ever? Please? The only difference is I have only had to hear about it for the last three weeks and she had to hear me ask her about ending the just dating thing for almost a year. How she handled that I will never know, but I knew I could not for that long. I looked down at the asphalt as my answer.

"That's what I thought." She too looked at the asphalt. My heart sank. I walked over and took her into my arms which she did not at first return. After what seemed like a lifetime she finally did, and then she kissed me. I was shocked, but allowed it, and then returned the kiss and pressed my body up against hers pinning her to her car. I moved to kissing her neck and eventually nibbling on her earlobe. She let out a soft sigh of approval. I did my best not to smile knowing she hated my self congratulatory grin. I was happy though in the fact that I still knew her weaknesses when it came to the physical part between us. She pulled me up by the back of my hair and looked into my eyes.

"Get in the car." She demanded in a quiet but serious tone. I let her go and ran to the passenger side of the car and hopped in as quick as I could. As soon as I did, we immediately started to kiss again tearing at each other's clothes, and then we made love.

18

"Don't you have to go?" Sarah asked me as we laid there together cuddled up as close as we could in her car. Still naked, and in that euphoric state that always follows intense moments of intimacy, I had lost all track of time and where I was supposed to be. Honestly, I did not care at that moment.

"Go?" I asked back in a dreamy sort of way staring into her perfect eyes.

She smiled. "Yeah, don't you need to be somewhere at 2:30?" As my senses started returning to me the realization of where I needed to be hit me. I sat straight up.

"Shit! What time is it?" I asked scrambling to find my watch. I had taken it off as it kept getting tangled in her hair. Sarah propped herself up on one arm and pointed out my watch to me.

"It's right there." I grabbed the watch and checked the time frantically. 2:45pm, it read. I was already 15 minutes late. I looked down at her and laughed then kissed her.

"I'm sorry, I've got to go" then added, "but I don't want to" kissing her again. She laughed, leaned over me and opened the car door.

"Get out. I'm late too." She said laughing. "I'm supposed to go shopping with my mom. Now look at me. I'm a mess." I looked at her, she was still perfect to me.

"You're beautiful." I said as seriously as I could.

"And you're blinded by what just happened. Now get out." She said in return still smiling. I kissed her one last time, grabbed my scattered clothes, and left her car.

I drove as fast as I could north on Rte. 2 to Sydney's place. I had no idea what I was going to say to her. I thought about stopping and calling her from a pay phone, but I decided against that as I thought it would be better to not lose the time. I could get her there in time if she did not make a big deal out of this before getting in the car. I pulled up to her house and my radio said it was 3:10pm. Fifty minutes to get to Catonsville was enough time I thought if I did 90 the whole way. I did not even have a chance to turn the car off before Sydney opened the passenger door and climbed into the car. She had already changed into her teams' uniform, I assumed to save time.

"Syd I'm so sorry I'm late" I said looking over at her. She did not look over in return.

"Drive" She replied in a disheartened tone.

I put the car in gear and sped off. I did my best impression of Mario Andretti weaving in and out of cars as I could. There were a few close calls, some horns honked at me, and the occasional middle finger sent my way, but all in all I thought I did well.

Sydney had a death grip on the "Oh shit" handle that resided on the interior roof on her side of the car, and she did not speak the entire time apart from muttering a few prayers, but other than it was fine, and I got her there by 4:10.

I dropped her off at the front door so she could head on in and then parked my car in the lot next to Kristi's. I made my way into the gym and saw Kyle waving down to me from the stands. I took the stairs two at a time and took the seat next to him. He looked me over and smiled.

"Jesus dude. You had one job today. One job." I looked over at him. "And you smell like Sarah." He said laughing a little while shaking his head. I smiled too.

"I couldn't help it." I said to him. He looked back over at

me and frowned a bit.

"You couldn't help it? She kidnap you and tie you up?"

"No. Nothing like that, but it was so incredible being with her like that again, I lost thought of everything else." He turned back to the court smiling then waved at Kristi. Sydney looked up as well, so I waved too. She did not return the sentiment.

"In the parking lot? In the middle of the day? Impressive." Kyle said responding to my statement.

"You think she knows?" I asked Kyle a little concerned.

"Of course, she knows. Maybe not to the full extent, but I'm sure she knows you were with Sarah and that's why you were late."

I thought about this for a bit while we watched the games start. It was a competitive match and in the end our team won, but I knew what I was going to do. I decided to love Sarah.

"I know what I need to do, but I don't know how without hurting her." I said to Kyle.

"It's about time! Sydney will be fine. She's tougher than you think."

We walked down to the court and waited for the girls to come over. Kristi walked over first waving to some people she knew still in the stands. Sydney was having a conversation with the coach. Her back was to us, but we could see her head nodding every so often. Kristi walked over to us, gave Kyle a hug, then back handed my chest.

"Nice job slick." She said to me smiling. "Jesus, you smell like Sarah." She added shaking her head. All I could do was smile in return.

19

This was working out perfectly. It could not have been any easier on me. I had, without trying, successfully pissed off Sydney without totally breaking her heart. It was just how I used to end things with girls I needed to move on from, piss them off and then have them dump me instead. That way they could save a little of their pride in the process. It was not until years later I had heard from our circle of friends that this was not the easy way for the girl. Whatever, it was happening yet again, and I did not care.

I had decided to take that chance with Sarah. Now I just needed to tell them both. I had not talked to either Sarah or Sydney since Thursday and the four-day break had been amazing on my mind. I had told Kyle and Kristi what I had decided back at the game, now it was time to make things happen.

I had successfully avoided Sydney all day at school. I wanted to talk to Sarah first. When I saw her waiting for me at the top of the commons, I decided that it needed to happen now. I made my way to her giving her a hug.

"Whoa. Aren't you worried about who will see?" She asked me a little surprised at the blatant public display of affection.

"Nope!" I replied shaking my head at her. "Damn the peasants." I hugged her briefly again. "Sarah, I need to talk to you." She looked down at her feet for a moment. She seemed a little nervous, and I do not mean the good kind of nervous, like first date nervous or first kiss nervous, but the other kind. The kind of nervousness that says "I'm going to destroy you and I'm sorry" kind.

"What is it?" I asked hesitantly. She looked back up at me and she looked full of sorrow.

"I met someone." We both stood there for a bit, me trying to decipher what that meant and her hoping not to need to go on.

"What do you mean? As in another guy?" Again, she looked down nodding her answer. I ran my hands through my hair.

"Oh my God! The timing is amazing. I was just going to tell you it was over with Sydney." I said laughing a little. Not out of humor, but out of trying not to go off the deep end. "When?" I asked her.

"Thursday, after you left." She said sheepishly. I said nothing forcing her to go on with what she needed to say. "We hung out Friday night, and again Saturday." I still said nothing, but she did not say anything after that.

"I'm assuming there's enough there that us being exclusive is not going to happen until you find out what this new guy may mean?" I asked with a slightly frustrated tone. She did not answer so I turned away from her.

"I didn't hear from you! Four days! Four! And not a word from you." She said in her defense.

"And when did you meet him?" I asked a little to heatedly.

"Thursday. After you left me." Her voice made it sound like it was my fault she met him. I could not believe what I was hearing. "He pulled up next to me at a traffic light. Then followed me. I stopped to get gas and we chatted."

"And that turned into a hang out." I guessed. She shook her head yes. I sighed. My world had just crumbled. Again. I knew now what I had to do. I knew I could not handle knowing Sarah was with someone else. I have been down that road before. I knew where it leads, and it was the one place I could not go back to. I started to walk away.

"Where are you going?" She cried out to me.

"Home Sarah, I'm going home."

"What does that mean?" I turned to face her before answering.

"It means look me up when you're ready for something real. Goodbye Sarah." I turned and made my way to the parking lot. I needed to find Sydney before it was too late.

20

I decided to head over to Kristi's before the drive home. I needed to talk to someone before talking to Sydney. It was a short drive to her house and on my way home and I was praying she was there and not out with Kyle. When I pulled up, I saw Kyle standing in the driveway leaning up against his car.

"Hey." I said getting out of my car.

"Before you go in you need to know Sydney is upstairs, she's pretty upset." He said in a serious tone as if it was meant to be a warning.

"Ok. Thanks for the heads up."

"Did you talk to Sarah?" He asked me again in the same tone.

"Yeah, that ship has sailed, I think. At least for now." He looked up to the clear sky and shook his head in disbelief.

"Oh my God why?" He asked not understanding how it went downhill so fast.

"It doesn't matter. I'll chalk it up to bad timing. For now." I moved closer to him, "Look, I need to know, how is Sydney? Did I screw this up too badly?" He sighed a long sigh.

"No. Not yet I don't think. For some reason she is hopelessly devoted to you. You could fix it. If you wanted to." I looked down at the ground. "But David, you've got to stop playing games with her. Don't string her along. If you're going to be with her then be with her." I knew what he meant, and he was right. I needed to move past Sarah Fulton.

"I know Kyle, I know. I'm ready." He smiled his huge grin

that drove all the girls wild. God, I hated that grin.

"Let's go find the girls." Kyle said escorting me around to the backyard.

We walked all the way to the end of the pier that went a good 50 ft out into the bay. At the end were some wooden chairs that sat facing the water. It made for some very pretty views in the mornings and evenings. Currently the sun was high and reflecting off the water which made for a beautiful view as well. I was instructed to take a seat and wait.

"I thought you said they were upstairs?" I asked Kyle a little confused as to why I had to wait here instead of going straight to Sydney.

"They are, but I think this scene gives you a better chance, and if she doesn't want to talk to you it avoids a scene inside with Kristi's parents being home." That certainly made sense to me. No use causing a scene. I sat there admiring the water and how the sun shimmered off the Bay. It really was a beautiful sight. I do not know how long I was sitting there staring out into the water, but I felt at peace and I knew I was smiling. Sydney's voice brought me out of my thoughts.

"David? Are you there?" She said in a quiet voice as if not wanting to disturb my thoughts. I do not know how long she had been there, but long enough to have taken the seat next to me.

I turned and looked at her "Your eyes are the greenest I've ever seen." I said to her in just as quiet of a voice. She smiled but only a little. I got the feeling that it was not what she expected to hear. Sydney turned her gaze out to the water. I followed suit.

"So? Are you done?" She asked me still using a quiet voice.

"Yeah, I'm done." I replied. She wiped a tear from her eye. I reached out and took her hand in mine which she reluctantly gave. "Sydney, with her I meant. I'm done with her." She stood from her chair and flopped down on my lap crying in relief. I wrapped my arms around her trying to let her know silently that everything would be ok.

"You hurt me." She said still crying a little.

"I know, and I'm sorry."

We sat there for a long time in silence, both of us looking out into the water. Still holding her I decided not to say anything until after she did. I would let her determine how this would play out and on her terms. I could wait until she was ready.

"You have to be done with her." Sydney said still looking at the water. I hugged her a little tighter as if forcing her to believe me.

"I am."

"I mean really done with her. No calls, no walks to the car, no nothing. Done." She said a little more emphatically.

"No more." I said trying to reassure her. After another long pause she asked me what I knew she would.

"Do you love me?" There was a little hint of hope in her voice, and despair as well. Hope in a confirmation so as not to feel like she was wasting her time and heart on me and despair knowing that I may never truly feel the same way about her as she does me. I said what I knew I had to in order to see where this relationship might go.

"I do." I said trying to sound as believable as I could. She turned back to me and hugged me.

"I so love you too." She said elongating the so. I felt awful for lying to her, but grateful knowing I would have the chance to find out. I knew I lied about a few things. One, I am never done with Sarah, but I could move on for now. And two, I did not love Sydney, not yet at least, but who knew what might happen with some time.

1992

21

I liked the winter at the beach. It was.......lonely. I know that seems a contradiction to my whole life until now, the struggles I have had with feeling alone, but this is different. The feeling of being lonely is vastly different than the feeling of being alone. There were maybe around a thousand people that lived in town during the winter compared to the near 2 million that visit Ocean City during the summer. It is quite a welcome relief. I would come home from work and be able to relax, minus the days that Kyle, Kristi, and Sydney would be here. Usually though, that would happen only on weekends. Monday through Thursday were still mine. I still drove back for school and volleyball, but the rest of the time was peaceful. I had a group of friends that were local and so would hang out with them as often as I could. One of which owned a surf shop and we had worked out a trade, surf lessons for bowling lessons. It was fun but neither of us really improved much with the help of the other. The water was too cold for me as well, so he got a lot more bowling lessons than I did surfing lessons. Surfing seemed not worth the effort from November until March because of how cold it was, but once mid-March rolled around, I found myself back in the water.

In April, I found myself receiving a full sponsorship to play beach volleyball. This year I would be hitting the east coast circuit without having to worry about any of the expense. Everything would be covered by the sponsor which was a welcome relief from trying to figure it out financially.

Things were good with Sydney. I did not feel anything more than what I had before, but I did not feel anything less either. I knew as Kyle started spending more and more time at the beach, as well as Kristi, the inevitable conversation with Sydney was going to have to happen. The "when can I move in too?" conversation.

"I don't get it. Why can't I?" Sydney asked sounding hurt and disappointed. "Don't you love me? You say you do whenever you're horny." She was not pleased with the way the discussion had been going and was starting to rant out of anger "Or is that just to get some kind of sexual gratification from me rather than masturbating? I'm sure you do a lot of that in the winter when I'm not here." Oh, she is feisty today I thought to myself. Kyle choked on the beer he was drinking out in the kitchen while listening to her vent. It amused him a bit even though he understood my reasons against her moving here. We have had this conversation, quite a few times actually, and it never seems to change except that she gets meaner and meaner in her arguments.

"Jesus Sydney. Yes, I love you. No, I don't tell you just to have sex, and yeah, I'm a 21-year-old guy, of course I do that when you aren't around." I said a little annoyed.

"Then why can't I move in with you here?" She asked almost yelling at me.

"We've been through this, and you've said you understood why." I said keeping my voice calm, but the frustration was setting in as well and with every word it was getting harder to maintain that calmness.

"Are you afraid I'll interrupt your ability to have other girls here? Or is it because you're still hung up on Sarah?" Now she was yelling and getting more and more angry by the second.

"Who? Wait. What?" I asked back not understanding this new argument of hers. Up until now she had never mentioned Sarah before. Sydney normally kept other girls out of her arguments whenever discussing this and she has never mentioned Sarah since that day on the pier at Kristi's house a few months ago.

"Sarah! You know that bitch you'd dump me for in a heartbeat if she gave you the time of day!" For someone as sweet as Sydney is she could sure turn ugly too. I knew I had made a mistake confessing that Sarah had come down last fall, but at the time I had thought the open and honest route, to a point, was best. I never told her about Sarah staying the night here, or the moment we had in the car, or any of the intimate moments we had shared, but I had confessed the lesser details. It had been months since she had used Sarah as an excuse to be mad at me. I had not even looked at Sarah since that day we had talked, and she told me about the new douchebag she had met at the traffic light. I could feel the anger swelling inside of me now, she knows that I do not do well with the accusations, especially if they involve Sarah.

"Is that so? You think I'm cheating on you?" She moved over closer to the front door as she was pacing back and forth from the fireplace to the door. She was kind of sexy though when she was mad, and I always liked her in the black leggings and sweatshirt she wore. She looked up at me scowling. Her green eyes radiated anger.

"No, but I know if she called, you'd answer." She said the words like they were poison in her mouth. She really hated Sarah without ever meeting her. Funny thing is I think they could have been friends under different circumstances. Kristi, hearing the argument, came down from their bedroom.

"What's going on?" She asked in a peaceful manner. She knew. She heard this argument about moving here all the time from Sydney. Kyle stayed in the kitchen, watching but chose to stay silent choosing to enjoy his beer rather than get involved.

"Same old same old. Syd thinks I don't want her to move in so I can cheat on her with Sarah." I said to Kristi in a mocking tone. Sydney continued her pacing, every now and then stopping to glare at me.

"Or any other slut." She added reaching the door again. That comment sent me over the edge. I felt no reason to be kind any longer. I looked up at Kyle and decided to let her have it.

"You know what Syd? If I'm going to be punished for something I didn't do, If I'm going to do the time" Kyle started shaking his head no and waving his hands to get me to stop. I turned back to look at Sydney and then finished my thought not caring that my words would hurt her. This argument had to stop, and for good this time. "Then I might as well do the crime. I'll call Sarah up and see what she's doing tonight." I finished with as cold of a tone as I could give. Kyle sank his head into his arms on the countertop not understanding at all why I would say such a thing.

Sydney let out a primal scream, grabbed the red rooster umbrella holder and threw it at me as hard as she could. I ducked without much effort as the rooster flew over my head and hit the wall shattering into a hundred pieces. Good I thought. One less hideous decoration to worry about.

"Oh no, not the rooster umbrella! Whatever will we do now without that beautiful accent piece?" I asked mocking her. Sydney screamed again and ran up the stairs. "Guess who's fixing the wall? And take a Midol while you're up there!" I yelled to her as I heard my bedroom door slam. I reached down and grabbed the Volleyball Monthly magazine resting on the coffee table and thumbed through the pictures inside unconcerned with the fight or how Sydney might be feeling.

"Dude, seriously? Did you have to go there?" Kyle asked coming in from the kitchen in a sympathetic voice. He seemed to be on her side for some reason. Kristi stood in front of me with her hands on her hips looking down at me in amazement.

"You really are an ass" she said. I could hear the silent fury in her voice.

"I'm sorry about making fun of the rooster, I know you liked it." I said trying to make amends with Kristi.

"Screw the rooster you dick! How can you be so heartless towards her?" She said pointing upstairs.

"What did I do? She started it with her accusations!"

"Yeah, all of which are true, and you know it. And so does she." Kristi turned from me and made her way up the stairs pausing halfway up. "Why did you have to throw Sarah in her face like that? Why couldn't you just have reassured her?"

"Because she's wrong. Sarah has nothing to do with her moving down here."

"Maybe not" Kristi turned back to the stairs "but we both know if it were Sarah here having this same conversation with but about Syd, you would have handled this a lot differently." She started walking up the stairs again "You would have loved her."

I looked over at Kyle. "You agree with her?"

He tilted his head as if in thought, "That was cold, even for you. Funny as hell to me, but cold." He plopped down next to me on the couch grabbing the Sega controller and turned the video-game system on then handed me the other controller.

"I mean, in a span of three sentences you told her you were going to hang out with Sarah tonight, insulted the stupid umbrella holder she loved, and demanded she fix the wall. All while not even being willing to discuss her feelings on an issue and then you blamed it all on her period! Ballsy. Funny as hell, but cruel."

I chose the character I was going to use for the game of golf we always played on the Sega and thought about his comments. Maybe I had taken it to a level it did not need to go. I blame my mother for this. We fought all the time and it seemed like the best way to end an argument was to say something cruel.

"I'll apologize later. Give her some time to cool off."

"You think that will be enough?" He asked. We played the game in silence; in fact, the whole house was silent. I could not hear anything that was happening upstairs. No talking, no crying, no movement, nothing. When the game ended, I set the controller down and made my way to the stairs.

"Good luck" Kyle said to me smiling. I got the feeling he did not think the next conversation would end well either.

"No luck needed. I know how to fix this."

"You're that confident?" He asked obviously not as sure as I was.

I started walking up the stairs "I bet I sleep with her." Kyle laughed then went back to his game.

22

I opened the door to my room and saw both girls sitting on my bed facing each other apparently in a deep conversation. Kristi looked up at me as I stood in the doorway, Sydney did not. She turned to face the wall as if not wanting to look at me. Kristi gave Sydney's knee a little pat to comfort her and then made her way over to me "You fix this." She said pointing her finger at me. I nodded my understanding. I understood she wanted me to make Sydney feel better, I was not going to admit I was wrong. I was not wrong, and as if reading my mind, she hugged me.

"At least make her understand." She said then walked past me and out of my room "Without hurting her." She added then went down the stairs and back to Kyle.

I looked over at Sydney, I could tell she had been crying. She looked a wreck. Well as much as someone as physically beautiful as she can look like a wreck. Her eyes were puffy and her nose red. Her hair had been pulled back into a ponytail and she had apparently been using one of my IEVB t-shirts as towel to wipe away her tears as I could see that there was makeup smudged on it.

"Sydney, you"

"Stop right there. If you don't start off with an apology you might as well go back downstairs" she said interrupting me. Sydney turned to face me gauging both my mood and thoughts. She must not have liked what she saw as her head turned back to face the wall.

"And I am not on my period" she added softly. I walked over and sat on the bed in front of her and took her hand in mine.

"I'm sorry for throwing Sarah in your face like that, and the Midol comment." She turned to look at me and could see in my face that I meant it. The expression on her face changed from pure sadness to one of hopefulness. Not happy, but hopeful that she may yet get her way.

"But as far as moving down here goes, I'm not sorry on my thoughts on that subject." She turned back away from me. "Syd, it's not that I don't want you here. It's not that I don't love you. You have a great opportunity at UMBC to go to school for next to nothing and play Division 1 volleyball. I can't let you waste that."

She turned back to face me. "Not even for the summer? Like Kristi and Kyle?" she pleaded. I shook my head no.

"You have off season stuff to do. You'll be gone most of the summer. Why feel obligated to a place that you can't be at but every now and then? Plus, your parents would disown you if said you were living here, and they would kill me."

Her head and shoulders sank a little. "I know. You're right. It just sucks with me being there and you here." She knew the truth of my words. This was not the first time we have discussed this, but I was hoping it would be the last. As I said, her arguments were getting meaner every time we would have this discussion and I was unsure how much more either one of us could take.

"Look Syd, you can come down every chance you get, stay for the part of the summer that you don't have to be at school if you like, come down every weekend, hell keep clothes here and other stuff if you want, I'll even give you your own key. We just won't label it as your living here. You are just visiting, but as often as you like."

She smiled at the thought and her mood brightened a little. "You'd do that for me? Let me keep stuff here and give me my own key? I can come down as often as I like, and you won't care?" She asked starting to get a little excited. Her eyes sparkled a bit as hope turned to reality.

"Yeah. I can do that for you." I confirmed knowing I had to compromise a bit. Her smiled widened and before I knew it, she threw herself on me kissing me hard and an hour later I had fulfilled my guarantee to Kyle.

23

The summer came and went much faster than I would have liked. Filled with endless days of surfing, work, and friendly evening hangouts. I played in as many volleyball tournaments as I could and got to go to some amazing beaches in the process. People may have discounted the Jersey Shores, but they were my favorites to visit. I liked them much better than the Florida ones. I am not sure why. The people were friendlier? I do not know, but I just did.

Kristi and Kyle were still in love as much as ever. Their playful banters, and Kyle's need to make her as happy as she could be, worked for them. I did my best to take the same approach with Sydney and it seemed to work for us as well. I kept my word. I gave her a key to my place and allowed her to come and go as often as she wanted. It was a little weird the first time I came home from work and she was there without me knowing ahead of time, but as the summer went on, I got used to it and even appreciated it. It was nice to see her so happy. I found myself not liking when she was gone and had begun to second guess my thoughts on her not living here. She seemed to go out of her way to make me happy as well. She cooked, which was something I was not used to since generally I was the one cooking. She cleaned, did laundry, I even came home and caught her putting flowers into a mulched area by the house. I did not ask her to do these things, or need her to, Sydney did them all on her own so that we could just "be" when I got home. It was thoughtful and genuinely nice on her part I thought. It is who she is.

We did everything together while she was in town and I felt as if my feelings for her were growing. I still did not "love" her, but I was getting close. Then August rolled around, and Sydney had to move on campus. Looking at her schedule we both knew that unless I made some trips to her there would not be but maybe a couple of days we would be together. This made me a little sad and our first day apart was dismal to say the least.

"Why are you moping like a little bitch?" Kyle asked me. "It's not like you love her or something." Kristi shot him a hot look. Seeing he had upset her he went back to making the spaghetti he was preparing for the three of us.

Sydney had left this morning to school, much to the relief of her parents who I think were starting to get a little worried that she would stay here instead. Their relief though was my sorrow and as if Mother Nature knew of my sadness, she, in her empathy, brought on the rain within an hour of Syd's departure. It was still raining even now at 6pm with occasional flashes of lightning and cracks of thunder.

"I like her though, and as strange as this may sound, I miss her." I said in the defense of my mood. Kristi looked at me taking in my demeanor.

"Maybe you do. You may love her." She said in a comforting voice.

"It doesn't feel like it. It's not like how it was with Sarah." She looked over at Kyle who was busy stirring the sauce and then back to me.

"Of course, it doesn't feel the same. It won't ever be the same." She leaned in a little closer so she could lower her voice. "Each time I've been in love it's been different." She stated hoping Kyle would not hear her.

"Really? And how many times has that been?" Kyle asked from the kitchen. She rolled her eyes as if saying "damn, he was not supposed to hear that." I laughed for the first time all day.

"Just twice my love." Kristi answered a little too condescending like. Kyle dumped the finished noodles into a strainer and took the garlic bread out of the oven.

"Twice? "Each time" Sounds like more than twice." He gave the air quotes for the words each and time and with the oven mittens on it looked kind of funny. Kristi stood from the couch and made her way out to the kitchen.

"Should I ask David how many times you've been in love?" She said looking at him while folding her arms across her chest. This was her standard defensive posture which signaled to everyone that knew her she was ready for a fight. Kyle took notice of her stance as well and, I could see he was trying to decide just how far he wanted this playful banter to go on.

"There's only been you babe." He said then gave his legendary grin. Kristi looked at me for conformation.

"We talking love? Like real love? I'd say you're at least number two. At least." I said answering her unspoken question. She turned back to him still holding her stance.

"Traitor." He yelled to me.

"Just keeping it real." I yelled back. Kristi dropped her arms then went over and wrapped her arms around him.

"What does it matter how many times? I love you now." She said trying to sweet talk him. "And the most." He hugged her back then kissed the top of her head. Then they parted and she walked back to me and took her place back on the couch. "The point is, each time has been different, each unique, and so never the same." I knew the logic she was using but I still was unsold on the idea. "You're expecting it to be the same and it won't be. Sarah will always be special because she was the first, but that doesn't mean Sydney is less, simply different." I thought about this. Maybe she has a point.

We moved to the kitchen table once Kyle announced that dinner was ready and then we started to eat. It was good, a little too much garlic, but good. It reminded me of the stereotypical bachelor cooking. Every guy does the same thing by trying to impress girls with their cooking skills, they feel the need to add way too many spices. Generally, garlic. The more the merrier. I do not subscribe to this kind of male cooking; I prefer to taste my food and accent it with spices rather than only taste the spices. To each their own, I guess.

"I don't know. I think you know when you're in love. You shouldn't need convinced that you are." Kyle said taking an opposing position while twirling his fork at his noodles.

"True. All I'm saying is that each time is different." She argued back as if defending her opinion. "Like food" she added. We both looked at her confused now. "You love lobster, right? And you love steak. Both are great, but unique, different." She added finishing her thought and then took a bite of spaghetti. Kyle and I both nearly choked as we laughed at her logic.

"What? It's true." She said defending herself. Then dropped her fork and folded her arms again over her chest when we did not stop laughing. "You two are assholes" she said as the laughter continued. Once we finally got control of ourselves Kyle piped in.

"Babe, I'm not arguing that it's different for each person you fall in love with, I'm saying you know when you know and shouldn't have to be convinced into it."

"Whatever." She said sounding hurt and then went back to eating.

"I think he does like her; he's grown used to her, comfortable. But there's a fine line between love and habit. It may not be love but just used to her being here, or around." Kyle said. That could very well be it I thought to myself. The phone rang interrupting our conversation and Kristi jumped up to answer it.

"Hello." Her face brightened as the person on the other end was talking.

"Yeah, he's here. Hold on one second." She set the phone down and looked over at me "It's for you." She was still smiling. I stood up and made my way to the phone. I could hear Kyle ask "Who is it?" to Kristi in a whisper. She did not answer but laughed her little laugh and shook her head. I checked my watch and thought it was a little early for Sydney to be calling. I knew her day was packed with moving in and volleyball stuff for school.

"Hello?" I said into the phone making it sound like a question. When the person on the other end began to speak, I cut them off mid-sentence.

"Hold that thought. Let me go upstairs. Give me a second." I set the phone down and ran up to my room.

"Now that's love right there." Kyle said pointing at me with his fork as I ran past them both.

24

How long had it been since I had talked to Sarah? Nine months maybe? Just long enough to move on again, but not long enough to forget. I took the stairs two at a time anxious to get up to the privacy of my room. I had not heard Kyle's comment, but I was sure it was something clever to gain the upper hand in the debate that had been taking place. When I made it to my bed, I grabbed the phone without taking the time to compose myself.

"Hi!" I said way too excitedly and slightly out of breath from the mad dash I had made to my room. Sarah laughed a little.

"Hi. You ok?" She asked noticing my gasps for breath and clearly amused knowing I had run up to my room to speak with her in private.

"Yeah! I'm great!" I answered wishing I could have caught my breath first. "How are you?" I asked after a moment of silence.

"I'm Ok. Getting ready to head to Frostburg for the semester." She said and I could tell by her voice she was smiling.

"Really? You're going to finish school at Frostburg?" My mind started swirling with all kinds of crazy thoughts. How was this going work for us? Wait, what us? I still believed, eventually, there would be an us. Now though? Did I really believe there would still be an us? Why hadn't I fought for us 9 months ago? I let her walk away yet again.

"Yeah, that's what I'm saying" she answered back. She could tell I was floundering.

"Wow" was all I could manage still trying to gain my composure from the sprint up the stairs. After a few moments of silence, she began to talk saving me from my inability to make conversation.

"So, I was wondering if I might be able to see you before I go? Maybe come down to the beach next weekend? If that's ok?"

"Yeah! That would be great! You could stay here if you'd like." Once again, I sounded overly excited. When did I become Weston? I quickly grabbed the calendar on my nightstand and checked the dates Sarah would be here and found it was a weekend that Sydney would be out of town with her team. I silently let out a sigh of relief.

"Ok, sounds good. Next Friday then?"

"I can't wait." I said in response. Wait what? I can't wait? You have not talked to this girl in 9 months and suddenly you cannot wait? Jesus, I do sound like Weston. Sarah laughed again.

"Bye David. I'll call you on Thursday to make sure everything is still fine for Friday. Talk to you soon" she said and then I heard the line go dead.

"Yeah, I can't wait" I stated into the phone knowing there was no one to hear me.

25

The week went by too slow for me. I was preoccupied with my thoughts of Sarah coming for a visit and I could not stand the agony of waiting. The weekend was setting up to be perfect as well since it seemed Kyle and Kristi would both be gone for a crab feast her mom had every year for her clients. I had been invited as well, and in past years I had gone and had a great time, but for obvious reasons I had declined the invite this time. Nothing could drag me away from the beach this weekend. Nothing.

I was lucky also in the fact that my conversations over the phone with Sydney had been short and brief. Never long enough for her to see how distracted I was, but long enough not to seem rude either. She was distracted with other things as well, so I am sure that helped take some of the pressure off me to make long conversation since I knew how busy she was. I was thankful that she was as busy as she was, and Syd would start every conversation with "I can't talk long I've got X, Y, or Z happening in a few minutes". I tried to sound as understanding as I could. I felt bad for her as I could tell she was stressed out and that she wished she were here, but there was not much I could do for her accept try to be as empathetic as I possibly could in my current distracted mindset. She would have to get by on her own, at least for this weekend.

Finally though it happened, and at 6:30pm the doorbell rang. I ran to the door and opened it as fast as I could and when I did, I took in the complete sight of Sarah. Her hair was longer than the last time I had seen her and blonder as if the sun had been highlighting her hair all summer. Her eyes were still the bluest I had ever seen, and her face was sun kissed with color. I did not get to look below her face before she walked into the house and closed the door behind her. We looked at each other in silence for just a moment and then as if neither one of us could control ourselves we both went into each other's arms and began one of those long slow soft kisses that seem to be only in the movies and that last forever.

"Who's here?" Sarah asked in a soft voice still under the euphoric feeling of the kiss. I opened my eyes and saw hers were still closed. Her mouth was still close to mine as well.

"No one. It's just you and I this weekend." I replied in the same tone of voice as hers.

She moved in closer and began another kiss only this time it was harder, more passionate, and with a different purpose. I matched her intensity as best as I could pulling her in closer with my arms allowing our bodies to press up against each other's. After what felt like an hour we separated. Sarah looked into my glazed over eyes and must have seen what she wanted to see as a small smile came over her face. She stepped back out of the embrace entirely, grabbed my hand and walked past me. Without saying a word, I followed her allowing her to lead me up the stairs and into my room. The last words spoken for the night were hers instructing me to close the door behind me.

26

The next morning, I could not wait for her to wake. My excitement level was high after the previous night and I could not sleep any longer. Unfortunately, I did not want her to sleep any longer either, but knowing she was not the best morning person I had decided to let her continue sleeping rather than risk her wrath and ruin the rest of the day.

When we had finally fallen asleep the night before we had done so facing each other, but somewhere in the night we had changed to "spooning". I had propped myself up on my elbow so I could look down at her and I was just as amazed today at her beauty as I was so long ago. I marveled at how her hair laid perfectly spread out across the pillow and yet not a strand seemed out of place. I could not help but think how I hate spooning, yet here I was enjoying every moment of it. The thought occurred to me that this seemed more comfortable with Sarah, like our body's fit perfectly together unlike with Sydney where it seemed awkward and not natural. I smiled at the thought and as if possessing some secret superpower Sarah noticed without ever opening her eyes.

"Quit that. You're making this weird." She said still facing away from me then pulling my loose arm around her tighter.

"Good morning to you too" I replied still smiling. Then I leaned down and kissed her exposed neck lightly.

"It can't be morning yet. What time is it?" I checked the alarm clock. When I saw the time, I knew she would not be happy. The shades in my room were closed and I had no idea it was still this early since no light was coming through them.

"Uhm, 5:15." I said in a meek voice knowing this might not go over well. A small smile appeared on her face, but her eyes remained closed.

"See? Not morning yet. Morning doesn't start until at least 9am on a Saturday."

"It does on your birthday" I said kissing her again hoping to pry her gently into waking.

"It's not my birthday" she replied still sounding half asleep.

"I know. It was Thursday the 13th."

"That was two days ago" she said starting to sound slightly annoyed that we were still talking instead of sleeping.

"I know. I was going to take you out last night to celebrate, but we didn't make it that far. So, it will have to be celebrated today."

"You could have told me Thursday when we talked to confirm this weekend. I don't remember you saying anything on my actual birthday." She said turning her head so she could see my face and my reaction. Oops. I guess I had not wished her a Happy Birthday then.

"I didn't. I'm sorry. I should have, but I was so excited about you confirming that you were coming it kind of slipped my mind until yesterday. Kind of selfish of me I know. Can you forgive me?" I replied in the sincerest voice I could muster. She turned her face back away from me and settled back into the spooning position pulling me closer.

"Good answer. Really good answer." She closed her eyes again and I could see she looked happy.

Sarah fell back to sleep with ease, me not so much. I tried, but at 6:30 I pulled myself away from her and went downstairs. I decided to cook her breakfast and make some coffee. I am not a huge coffee person, but I like it on weekends. I had no idea if Sarah liked coffee or not, but I would make enough for her as well just in case.

Unsure of what she liked for breakfast, since it had been a couple of years since the last time we had shared a breakfast together, I decided on scrambled eggs, French toast, some blueberries and cantaloupe, and sausage. I figured there was bound to be something there she would eat. Lacking actual serving trays because I am only 21 and who owns that kind of thing at 21? I loaded up her plate onto a cookie sheet along with a glass of Kristi's OJ and a cup of coffee.

When I opened the door, I noticed her eyes were still closed so I set the tray down on the nightstand next to her side of the bed and then crawled in bed next to her hoping I would not wake her.

"Mmmmm. Is that coffee?" She asked smiling a little smile.

"It is, along with breakfast too."

"You made me breakfast? I get breakfast in bed?" Her voice was both excited of the thought of someone making breakfast for her and still groggy from not wanting to be awake yet. A cute and interesting mixture I thought to myself.

"Happy Birthday."

She pulled me tighter and then started to press her body against mine. She was still naked, and the result of her touch did not go unnoticed.

"I've never had breakfast in bed before." She pressed her body against me even harder. "I can tell you're awake." Once again, the smile appeared on her face. She rolled over onto her back extending her body outward in a long stretch. The blanket stayed in place and as she stretched, her body extended past the top of the blanket exposing her breasts. I took in a brief glance of her exposed form which caused even more of an aroused state.

"Like what you see?" She asked me slyly apparently catching me checking her out.

"I've always thought you were the most beautiful person in the world." She studied me for a moment as if judging my sincerity. I decided to lighten the mood a bit. "Eat your breakfast, we need to get going."

She sat up and did not bother covering herself up seeming to be in complete comfort, or she just liked knowing I was trying my best not to attack her I'm not sure which, but once propped up I handed her the tray of food and beckoned her to eat. I was pleased when I saw her start with the French toast, at least I got one thing right.

"What's the plan for the day?" She asked before taking another bite. My eyes went to her still exposed and perfect boobs.

"Hey. My eyes are up here." She said to me smiling. Please, I thought, you know exactly what you are doing to me.

"Sorry. I thought head to the beach for a while, then Bull on the Beach for a late lunch, and maybe Seacrets for the night?" I tried to sound as if her body was no longer on my mind. I was positive I failed in that regard.

"I'm 19!" She said protesting the Seacrets idea. She did however pull the blanket up high enough to remove the distraction of her form from my eyes.

"I can get you in. Or would you rather do something else?" She thought about it for a moment and her face took on an expression of serious thought as if going through the options.

"How about the boardwalk tonight? You know, some Thrasher's Fries? Milkshakes? Boardwalk games? Maybe even the rides? Like we used to do?" She asked in a shy kind of voice. I could tell this was really what she wanted but was thinking I might consider it too touristy.

"Mini Golf too?" I asked her back wanting to allay her fears of doing touristy stuff. She smiled in return at the idea. "If that's what you want to do? It's your birthday weekend. I'm good with it."

She got excited and sat up even straighter. "So, I can ask for anything? We'll do anything I want?"

I nodded my affirmative answer. She moved the tray of food back to the nightstand and then pulled me hard to her and kissed me. Every moment, every kiss was more intense than the last and I found myself pulling away from her.

"What's wrong?" She asked with a disgruntled look on her face.

"Nothing! Nothing at all, I'm just anxious to start the day with you."

"What? I'm trying to start the day with you" She said in response emphasizing the I'm.

"I'm sorry, I meant out with you. I'm excited to show you a great day."

She kicked the blanket off her and stood up from the bed and stood in front of me naked "You are such an idiot sometimes. If I'm throwing myself at you like that then I must have wanted to. It sounded like a great way to start off my birthday weekend to me."

She started walking away from me and the bed and I thought about what she said. I must be crazy, why would I pull away from that? I reached out to grab her arm to try and pull her back to the comfort of the bed. Maybe get another chance?

"No" she said in a mocking tone. "That ship has sailed." She laughed still mocking me. "I'm going to jump in the shower." She made her way to my bedroom door and opened it. I looked down at my bed feeling stupid and wondering how I could have screwed that up so badly. I wanted this perfect birthday week-end of events for her, and I have already screwed up 30 minutes into it. She called back to me from the bathroom "If you want to come wash my back though, I think I'd allow that." I jumped out of my bed and ran to the bathroom as fast as I could.

27

It was the most incredible day. I could not have dreamed of a better one. For so long I had wished for just one more perfect moment with Sarah and today I felt like we finally had it. We had made it to the beach by noon. There was no sun tanning quietly in chairs, no, for us it was a long walk up the beach searching for perfect shells for Sarah to make jewelry with sprinkled with the occasional dip into the water. Twice she found amusement in pushing me into an oncoming wave hard enough for me to lose my balance and go completely under. I acted upset, or shocked, but I was not mad. How could I be when I saw how happy she was and how amused she was with herself?

For lunch we opted for steamed shrimp choosing to share 1lb orders at a time. By 6pm we were home taking showers to get the salt and sand off our bodies where once again she had requested help with her back. As she had suggested we had finished the evening off at the boardwalk indulging in all her favorite foods and activities. At 1am we were back at home sipping on some wine. The night was cool enough for a fire, so here we were, sitting out on my back deck, using the firepit, and looking into each other's eyes. I had even let her win in mini golf thinking that would help make her birthday somehow more special.

"Oh my God! David Anderson, you did not let me win!" Sarah exclaimed her face turning serious. I laughed which made her even more upset. "David! Say that isn't true." Now she seemed hurt, so I stopped laughing. I decided to lie.

"OK. Ok. Ok. I didn't let you win." She eased back down against my chest and back into my arms. We were sharing a lounge chair propped up enough to see both the fire and out into the bay. Upon hearing me say that I had let her win she had sat up to look down at me attempting to see if I was telling the truth. I was not expecting her to be so upset by it. She has always had a healthy competitive streak in her. That is not true, she has always had a competitive streak with me and me only. I never knew why, so I guess the idea of being "allowed" to win did not sit well with her.

"I'm not sure I believe you" she said quietly. Hearing her unsure voice of my sincerity I thought I would convince her of the lie. I did not want anything to ruin this weekend for her.

"I swear. You won fair and square." If I were a wooden boy my nose would have grown at least 3 inches by now. I kissed the top of her head.

"Thank you for today. It was a great birthday." She said switching topics. I could not tell if she believed me or not about the mini golf, but I decided to let it go as I assumed her topic change meant she was as well.

"Even though your birthday was Thursday?" I asked teasing her a little.

"We couldn't have done this Thursday so this year my birthday is Saturday August 15th instead." We laid there quietly for a while, her watching the bay and me deep in thought while playing with her hair. The thought occurred to me that we could have celebrated Thursday if only she was here.

"Sarah, do you have to go?"

"Not until tomorrow"

"No that's not what I meant" I said cutting her off "Do you have to go to Frostburg right now? Can it wait a year? Transfer as a Junior instead of as a Sophomore?" She sat up and looked at me not understanding yet.

"David what are you asking me?" I sat up too as if somehow it would add to the seriousness of what I wanted to ask her.

"Sarah, I love you; I've always loved you. I'm asking you to stay one more year, just one, and live here, with me." I was pleading with her. I have always known my life is better with Sarah in it than without her. I wanted as much time as she was willing to give and her moving here would be perfect.

"Oh David. I don't know. How will that work?" She asked back. Her voice was interested in the idea and concerned with it as well.

"Do another year at AACC. Transfer to Frostburg next fall. Stay here with me until then. At the beach." I pleaded.

"With you? Here?" She asked making sure she understood.

"Yeah. With me." I started caressing her back hoping my gentle touch would add to my request. She thought about it. Seriously thought about it.

"What about your girlfriend?" She asked back clearly knowing there were loose ends I would need to take care of and quickly for this to be a reality.

"I'll take care of that tomorrow morning first thing." A small part of me was dying inside knowing that this would crush Sydney, but if it meant a chance with Sarah then it had to happen.

"Where will I work?" Sarah asked me trying to find some reason that would make sense to say no.

"I know people, we can find you a job easily enough." She looked into my eyes and saw the truth in them.

"What about my parents?"

"Not enough room for them to move in. Sorry."

She smiled "You know they'll hate this?"

"Yeah, I know. But they'll get over it. As long as you go next fall for sure." She shook her head at me as if completely amazed.

"Damn. You have all the answers, don't you?" I kissed her.

"No. I only know that I love you and that I want you here. I'm not ready for you to leave again." She pushed me back down and then we assumed the positions we had been in, her laying in my arms and me playing with her hair.

"Can we talk about this tomorrow? It's a lot to think about?" She asked.

"Sure. I'm not going anywhere. Hopefully, you won't either." I said pulling her tighter to me. I could tell by her breathing she was relaxed and soon that relaxed state turned into the limpness that precedes sleep. I whispered goodnight to her and her final words before drifting off for good were "Now he fights for me."

28

"What's wrong?" Sydney asked in an exhausted voice. "It's not even 6am which means you either did something you need to apologize for or your horny. Those are the only times you call me this early in the morning. And I'm hoping your apologizing because I'm way too exhausted to deal with you being horny."

I had not been able to sleep. Sarah and I had made our way up to my room around 3am and after another hour of kissing each other goodnight I had finally allowed her to go to sleep. I unfortunately was not so lucky. I was too wound up, too excited in hope that Sarah would agree to put off Frostburg for a year and move down here with me. Either way though, I had to get this out of the way.

"Syd, I'm not horny, and I didn't call to apologize."

"Then what's wrong? I'm tired and want to go back to sleep. Sunday is the only day I can sleep in." I hated doing this. I hated breaking up with girls. It is so much easier to get them to break up with me. I decided I would just rip off the Band-Aid fast hoping it would sting less.

"Sydney, I need a break. We need a break. I need to get" The phone went silent on the other end and then I heard the dial tone. I did not even get to finish my thought. I guess that worked out as about as perfect as it could get for me. I should not be smiling, but I was. I decided to make some coffee and take a cup up to Sarah as well. Ten minutes later I walked into my room and placed her cup on the nightstand.

"Do you ever sleep?" She asked in a groggy voice. I tried

to appease the morning monster by kissing her head and then crawled back into bed next to her.

"I crash."

"Well, I sleep. And what the hell does that mean? "I crash?"" She asked in a slightly irritated tone. It made me smile.

"It means that I don't sleep much until I get so exhausted, I'll sleep for 12 hours straight." I answered back as sweet as I could manage. She was frowning and her eyes were still closed.

"That phone call was quick." She said changing the subject. Was I that loud? How did she know? "Yes. You were that loud." She said as if reading my thoughts.

"It was quicker than I thought it would be." Her frown changed to an exceedingly small smile.

"And?" She asked.

"It needed to happen. Whether you say yes or not. I can't be with her when I'm still so in love with you." She turned over and opened one eye to look at me, the other eye still too sleep filled to open.

"Hm. You always had a way with words," She rolled back over away from me "It's your actions that have always scared me." I thought about this for a moment. She was right. I have tended to be quite destructive to myself and to our relationship in the past.

"That was a long time ago." The phone started ringing which could be only one person "And I think my actions this weekend should say quite a bit." I climbed over her, kissed the side of her temple, and made my way down the stairs knowing Kristi would keep calling until I answered the phone.

"How pissed is she?" I asked into the phone forgoing the hellos. I knew it was Kristi. I knew Sydney would call her right away.

"Not at all actually. She just wanted to know if I knew you

were going to do that, which thank God I didn't. I take it that you and Sarah are having a good time?" Kristi sounded quite awake I thought considering it was still so early in the morning.

"Yeah. A great time actually." I answered. I noticed Sarah walking down the stairs. She had managed to find one of my Quiet Storm sweatshirts and had pulled her hair into a side ponytail. She wasn't wearing anything from the waist down, but my sweatshirt was long enough on her to cover everything that needed covered.

"Is she awake?" Kristi asked me as Sarah sat down next to me on the couch leaning herself against me. I wrapped my left arm around her as she sipped her coffee.

"She is. Sitting here next to me actually."

"Put her on the phone." I handed Sarah the phone and she took it a little reluctantly.

"Hello?" She said her voice still not working fully.

"Hi! Are you having a good birthday weekend?" Kristi asked way too excitedly for not even 7 o'clock on a Sunday morning.

"Other than David not letting me sleep at all it's been great." She smiled at me as she spoke.

"Will you still be there when Kyle and I get back tonight?"

"Maybe, what time will that be?" Sarah asked.

"6pm maybe at the latest?"

"Yeah, I can wait. I'll see you then." She handed me the phone.

"Ok Kristi, I'm hanging up now. We'll talk when you get back." I could hear her protesting as I set the phone back on the receiver ending the call. We sat in silence for about an hour when Sarah finally broke the silence.

"So, I have conditions." I smiled. That was a good start.

"Ok. Like what?" She sat up and sat on my lap straddling me so she could look at me.

"If I say yes, it's just for the year. Next fall I have to go to Frostburg."

"I know."

"This weekend, it's been amazing, but if I live with you this weekend won't be the reality. This won't be how it really is." She said with a genuine concern in her voice.

"How do you know? Have you lived here before?"

"No, but we'll be working, have real life stuff to do, household chores, stuff like that."

"True, but there will be plenty of times like this too."

"I'm not saying that I'm saying it will be different. I need to know that if trouble happens you won't go off the deep end, that you'll still be here, you will work things out between us and not run off to Dundalk." I laughed at the comment, she did not.

"I promise. I won't go off the deep end." She looked down at my chest not wanting to look me in the eyes.

"I can't do it full time. I'm not driving back and forth on school days, but I could do Thursday evening until Tuesday morning. I'll stay with my parents Tuesday through Thursday morning."

I was smiling one of Kyle's huge grins. "Ok, but when you're here, working or not, we have to have at least one meal a day together." I said giving her my condition of her living here. Now she was smiling.

"I don't want to be left behind either. I don't need to do everything with you, but I'm not going to be an afterthought either." She said.

"I'll take you everywhere I go if you want." My voice was filled with sincerity. I wanted nothing more than to spend as much time with her as I could.

She leaned in and hugged me "And one more thing?"

"Yes?"

"I'm not like you. You need to let me sleep. I don't do well without sleep. And you need to sleep too!" She said in a weary voice. I could tell the lack of sleep for the weekend was catching up with her.

"You are so demanding. Are you going to be this difficult about everything?" I asked teasing her.

"Probably." She answered flatly.

"Fine. I'll let you sleep." She hugged me tighter as if giving me her answer in the form of an embrace.

29

The rest of the summer was great with Sarah living here at the beach. It was only 6 weeks, but those 6 weeks were the best that a guy could ask for. Sarah had quickly found a job as a waitress slinging crabs at an All You Can Eat joint. Long hours, but great money. She worked 3 of the five days she stayed at "our" place and had two days off to enjoy herself. I did not alter my schedule for her, opting to keep it as life like as possible to show her it could still be great and not the fantasy world she had been used to with her past visits. It worked out fantastically. She had some free time to herself and we still had plenty of time for each other as well.

As she had suspected her parents were not thrilled with her being here. When they came to visit though they were still friendly keeping any conversations of their concerns to themselves or voicing them to Sarah only. Never did they speak of it in front of me. Work was starting to slow down for her though as the season was ending and part of me worried a bit as to what she would want to do once the work stopped.

October, to me, was the best time of the year at the beach. You had the whole town to yourself until Friday, and then Friday through Sunday afternoon the town was lively and packed with visitors. Still warm enough to enjoy the outdoors, but vacant to all but those that lived here.

"I still can't believe you live here." Kristi said watching Sarah clean the kitchen. The first weekend in October and Kristi had started her Friday night drinking early. Kyle and I had been enjoying a few games of Mortal Kombat on the Sega system while Kristi sat nearby watching Sarah.

"Oh, finish him!" Kyle screamed out as he beat me in the third game. I set the controller down as he set about putting the finishing move on my character.

"Why's that?" Sarah asked back smiling while wiping down the counters.

Sarah and Kristi had hung out quite a bit over the last 6 weeks. Whenever Kyle and I were working the two of them would head out together sometimes not getting back until well after the both of us were home from work. That became video game time for us. A few times the girls would return from the flea markets with new decorations for around the house. I thought the rooster umbrella holder was bad, but the one in shape of a pig carrying the umbrella was even worse. It even came with a matching lamp.

"Not so easy to say how ugly it is when you actually care about the person who bought it now is it?" Kyle had remarked when I fumbled with answering the question of if I liked it or not. Yeah, no. I thought it was uglier than the previous one shaped like a rooster. I could not tell her though since she seemed pleased with it.

"Oh I don't know, it's just different with you here, more fun, not like when" Kristi trailed off as if not wanting to speak Sydney's name. "Well, it's just better, more relaxed, and David is happier." I shot her a look that said "Really? you have to go there right now?" Sarah let the comments slide.

"Thanks. I'm glad I'm here too" she replied. Kristi looked back over at me.

"Why aren't you helping her?" She asked me with a disgruntled look on her face.

"I cooked remember? The chicken with crab imperial doesn't ring a bell? You said you liked it." I answered Kristi in return.

"You should still help her" she retorted back. I stood up to go and help thinking she was right, and it would be a nice thing to do.

"It's ok! He did cook and I'm almost done." Sarah said in my defense.

"Why are you giving me crap? Kyle never helps clean after dinner and he doesn't cook either unless it's some creative dish involving Ramen" I said to Kristi pointing at Kyle as I did so.

"Oh wow. Did anyone get the number of that bus?" Kyle asked still playing his game. Kristi turned to look at him now and smacked his thigh.

"That's true! Why aren't you helping?" He looked over and gave his best seductive smile that I hated.

"But Babe, I'm playing this game at the moment. I would've helped in a bit if she waited." She stared at him in disbelief. His grin continued as if hoping the magical spell that surrounded it would take effect. It was not.

"I'm going to start some laundry, which includes your stuff, are you going to help me?" She asked him.

Still the grin. "Babe, it's Friday evening, forget the chore type stuff, let's just enjoy the evening and worry about it sometime later this weekend."

Still the stare. You could feel the tension building in the room. How he missed that this was obviously a test I do not know, but he was failing miserably.

"You know you have no clean underwear for tomorrow?" She asked.

"I like going commando every now and then." He answered.

"Guys, I'm finished. Really no need to start anything. Who's in the mood for some frozen drinks?" Sarah said from the kitchen as if sensing the buildup as well. Ever the peacemaker I thought to myself.

"I'll do a slush." Kristi answered still staring at Kyle. The slush drink was a mixture of OJ concentrate, Lemonade concentrate, and vodka. Sarah would sometimes add rum as well. They were quite tasty and an easy drink to have as you did not taste the alcohol. Sarah went about the task of making the drinks. Doing so as quickly as possible as she was still trying her best to defuse the situation.

"I won't have any underwear for tomorrow either." Kristi said to Kyle in a more agitated tone.

"Oh wow. The idea of you going commando is kind of sexy. It's kind of turning me on a little I won't lie." Kyle answered back. Sarah hurried in handing the drink to Kristi and then took a seat next to me on the two-person loveseat.

"Cheers" Sarah said with a smile and took a sip then offered me a taste as well knowing the glasses she used were enough for two people to share. Kristi took a long drink, her eyes never leaving Kyle. Kyle on the other hand turned back to his game. Just how oblivious is he I thought to myself.

"This is really good." Sarah said taking another drink still hoping for a peaceful resolution.

Still the stare.

Still the game.

Kristi took another long drink. I could tell the alcohol was starting to kick in. She finally stood, wobbled a bit, then regained her poise turning to continue the stare. She turned to face him more directly blocking part of his view of the TV. He then leaned around her and then seeing that was not much help paused the game and looked up at her. Sarah finished her drink, as did Kristi.

"I'll go pour us another round." She said darting off into the kitchen and in short order was back with the drinks. Kristi took a long pull from her new drink. Sarah did as well returning back to her seat next to me. I took hold of her hand and placed it in her lap as she draped her legs over my lap lounging back a bit. I felt like eating some popcorn would be good while watching this drama unfold but was too nervous to make some.

Still the stare.

"You going to stand there all-night babe? I can't see my game." He asked her. She turned away from him and made her way to the stairs. As she passed by the TV, she pulled the power strip plugged into the wall out of the socket turning off the TV, and videogame system, in one quick motion. Kyle stood up in shock.

"Babe! What the heck?"

She made her way up the stairs. "You are about as useful as a vibrator with dead batteries." The next sound that was made was the closing of the bedroom door.

Kyle turned to me, still holding the videogame controller. "This is your fault." He said to me. Sarah snorted sending slush drink out her nose and coughing a bit.

"Me? How is this my fault?" I asked confused knowing darn well this was in no way my fault.

"You couldn't just let her complain about you for a few minutes. She would've dropped it eventually, but no, you had to divert her focus to me." He dropped the controller allowing it to hit the floor and then made his way up the stairs.

"Well," I said looking at Sarah "I guess you'll be hitting the flea markets tomorrow."

"Why's that?" She asked.

"Kristi always likes to go shopping after they've had an argument." I answered. A few moments later Kyle came down the stairs carrying a laundry basket full of clothes. He set to the task of putting a load into the washer and when he was finished, he looked over at us "Don't say a fucking word."

1993

30

Seasons change, and so do people. Well person I should say. I have always struggled with depression, everyone knows this. Some days I manage well, others not so much, but the colder and darker it gets the harder it is to control. So it was with this year as well.

Oh, the fall was beautiful. Full of many magical memories that I will never forget. Sarah running down the beach, Sarah planting mums in some pots on the back deck, Sarah washing her car on a warm day in December. Thanksgiving. Christmas. The New Year's kiss we shared. All such happy events, but then the new year starts, and you find yourself alone one cold dark Tuesday night, and it gets hard to keep the demons at bay.

It always starts so simple. A few drinks by myself, which turns into a few nights of drinks by me. Then it is late-night calls to Sarah that end with complaints about wishing she were here. It always starts out flattering, but a few months of this and it turns into accusations and demands. "Why aren't you here?" and "If you loved me, you'd be here." Before you know it even when she is here it just feels like pressure and neither of us are fun to be around. Oh, sure we would talk it out and make up, but eventually those talks get less and less sincere and all too frequent. By the end of March, we were officially done yet again. A little break we called it. Those little breaks though add up and when you have done this before with the same person both people lose trust in the other to choose love. The inevitable consequence is to look for it elsewhere. Sarah confessed to me one day in April that she had a date with someone and that she would be seeing him again.

That was a bad blow to me. So much so that when I left her at the community college parking lot I drove straight home and did the one thing I am good at attempting, but not great at achieving. I grabbed a butcher knife and had at my left wrist. I did not get far. Maybe 3 strokes? And I had been drinking the whole way home, so it took me a little longer getting home than normal which allowed Kyle and Kristi to catch up to me.

Sarah had apparently called Kristi thinking I might do something crazy, or harmful. Sarah knew me better than anyone, but she has never been around to see just how bad it can get.

"Shit. Shit. Shit! Grab the knife Kyle. I'll get a towel." Kristi yelled excitedly. I was crying. I do not remember when I started crying, but the tears were fast and plentiful. As Kyle once again wrestled a knife away from me, I sank to the floor and continued my heart broken sobs.

Kristi made her way back into the kitchen carrying a few towels with her. She quickly tied one off above the elbow as a makeshift tourniquet and then took a spot on the floor pulling my head onto her lap. She embraced me in a hug as best as she could from her position above me and applied pressure to the wounds. She rocked me back and forth like a mother would attempting to console a troubled toddler.

After the bleeding stopped Kyle checked underneath the towel to judge the extent of the damage. Kristi looked up at him trying to gauge his reaction.

"He's ok. Superficial wounds. Not too deep. Might need stitches, but nothing more." Kristi nodded her understanding. I had finally stopped sobbing, but I could still feel tears running down my face. It occurred to me that my eyes had been closed the whole time. I had not actually seen Kristi or Kyle yet. I was shifted from one lap to another. This lap felt different from Kristi's and yet somehow familiar.

"You would think you'd be better at this by now" Kyle said with a hint of humor in his voice. I could feel him smiling. It made me chuckle a little which of course made me snort and send snot and spit everywhere.

"I mean you kind of suck at killing yourself" He added.

"Jesus Kyle!" Came Kristi's voice along with "Stop it!" from another voice I recognized all too familiarly.

"I'm just saying" Kyle added. I knew he was trying to lighten the mood. He knew, as well as I did, that the moment had passed. He knew I was not going to stand up and try again no matter how much I wanted to. Not while everyone was here at least.

"Sydney?" I asked in a hoarse voice. She stroked my head brushing hair back in a gentle calming motion.

"Yeah. I'm here." She replied in a soft gentle voice. She sounded concerned and caring at the same time. I hugged her legs and waist as if they were the only thing keeping me afloat in an open violent ocean, but I did not speak. Kristi must have felt she needed to offer up an explanation to fill the silence.

"Sarah called after you left her."

"From a payphone." Kyle added.

"Right. And well we were actually hanging out with some of the girls from the old volleyball team at my house and we told everyone we needed to leave right away". She went on "we didn't say why." She added as if to alleviate any concerns of the peasants knowing my personal issues.

"Or where" Kyle added once again.

"We just left my house. Sydney walked us out to the car

because she was concerned. I didn't say why we needed to get to you, just that we did as quickly as possible."

"David, you've told me before about your, well struggles, in the past and I was worried. I wanted to help if I could and if you'd let me." Sydney broke in feeling the need to explain why she was here.

"Anyways, we didn't think it could hurt and we may have needed her help." Kyle put in. I hugged Sydney once again. She was exactly what I needed at that moment, that feeling of knowing you are loved unconditionally. Sydney excelled at that, at least with me.

"Please don't be upset with them that I am here." She said continuing the soothing strokes to my head. I felt as if those little motions were keeping my head from exploding. She was a comfort to have now. Where one of Sarah's faults may have been to run away from me anymore once the going gets a little tough Syd's was, for the most part, one to embrace the challenge and try to work things out as best as she could. She never would have left me. I was the one that ended things with her in order to have the chance to see where things might go with Sarah. Now I know.

No matter how crappy I had treated her, she stayed. I may not have ever loved her the way I should have, but that was never one of her issues. Sydney had always shown me nothing but love.

"I'm not mad. I'm glad you are here. A little surprised, and really embarrassed, but I am glad you are here." I said in as calm a voice as I could muster.

I could hear Kristi sigh a little and feel her tension ease. I think she finally realized I was over the hump. At least for the time being. Who knew what tomorrow would bring? Pills mixed with alcohol? Jumping in front of a moving vehicle? Maybe a dive off a balcony from one of the high-rise hotels in town? Save tomorrow for tomorrow I guess, think about today instead.

After a few long minutes of silence Sydney decided to release the rest of the tension in the air. "I like what you've done with the place. That pig umbrella holder is so much better than the rooster one. And it came with a matching lamp? Genius!" We all laughed at the comment, and just like that, the final touches had been done returning us all back to a sense of normality.

I pushed myself up from her and felt a little lightheaded. I looked at my arm and noticed the gashes. Too far to the left of my arm I thought, and it would need stitches.

"Ok. Can we take this to the living room? I'm getting cold on this floor. And Kyle will need to tape this up for me."

Sydney looked confused. "Tape"?

"Yeah. Can't go to a Doctor or ER. They'd want to hold him. So, tape can work like stitches. You just change it every other day or so. Eventually though the wound heals." Kyle answered.

They helped me up and walked me to the couch. I resumed my position with my head on Syd's lap on the couch while Kyle and Kristi took the smaller sofa. Someone placed a blanket over me, and I could feel myself falling asleep.

"Rest David. We're all here for you" I could hear Sydney say, but my last thoughts were of Sarah. Of her blue eyes and of her smile, and how I felt crushed by her once again, and with that thought tears fell once again from my eyes.

31

May came and left and with every day I felt better. Sydney never left. She stayed by my side the whole time. Well, most of the time. I still worked and she obviously could not come with me to work, but she did drive me there and would pick me up when I was done. She was a great friend. Nothing physical happened between us. We did not hold hands. We did not kiss. We did not share a bed or anything like that, but she was always there. She never pushed for more, or less for that matter, she just was there when I needed her. Sometimes I would cry, and she would console me. Sometimes I would shake with an uncontrollable coldness, and she would hold me and try to warm me up. Sometimes I would be lost in silent thought as if contemplating all of life's great mysteries, and she would wait to speak until she knew I was ready. She was everything I needed at any given moment but required nothing of me in return.

Her green eyes were still as mesmerizing as ever and her hair had not changed from when we were together. She was still just as beautiful as she ever was but somehow sweeter if that were possible. I knew I could love her. One day. Under the right circumstances. It just was not that day yet. Not because she lacked something, or failed in some way, or had some hidden flaw, but only because my heart, for some ungodly reason, still belonged to Sarah.

In June, an unexpected, but much needed, visitor came to town. His huge smile and exceedingly loud laugh filled the house when he walked in through the front door. I had heard the knock, but it was Kyle who had sprung up from his seat that Saturday morning to answer it. Kristi was reading some girly magazine while Syd, sitting next to me in a darker green bikini top that accented her eyes, and white shorts, was also reading some other girly magazine.

"Huh, 10 ways to make sure he doesn't stray. Interesting." Sydney said not realizing that someone had walked into the house.

"I should read that when you're done." Kristi said not looking up from whatever junk she was reading. Me? I was just staring out the backdoor looking out across the bay thinking of nothing and yet everything at the same time. Ohio entered my mind. How long had it been since my last visit? I missed my aunt's farm. Shoenbrunn too. For some reason candlelight services at Shoenbrunn specifically. How long had it been since I had been there?

"It's called a Blow Job." Kyle yelled from the front door.

"Gross" Kristi muttered under her breath clearly disgusted by his comment.

I heard the unmistakable laugh. "What's called a Blow Job?" the familiar voice asked Kyle.

"10 ways to make sure your man doesn't stray. I guess you can't sell magazines though if you give them the only real way." Kyle answered back confident in his relational advice.

"Asshole" Kristi muttered again.

"Oh" the familiar voice said in response to Kyle and then the laugh again. I sat up quick when I heard that stupid laugh that brought me out of my thoughts of Ohio.

"Weston?" I asked to no one in particular. Weston and Kyle entered the living room.

"What's up bitches?" Weston asked smiling at us all. I ran to him and embraced him hard. How long had it been now? Two years? Three? I have only spoken to him here and there since he had followed that girl to Austin, Texas. I could not allow myself to let go of him and as if understanding he did not force me to but allowed the embrace to go for as long as I needed.

"I'm so glad you are here." I whispered to him while still hugging him with my head still buried into his shoulder. He patted my back a little.

"I know. I know. I'm here now." I allowed the embrace to end and wiped the tears of joy away from my eyes.

"How long are you staying?" I asked still in shock that he was here. Kristi and Sydney stood and came over to greet him.

"As long as he wants. He's going to use the small room." Sydney answered. I looked over at her in shock. I could not believe what they had just told me. I was so happy to hear this.

"If that's ok with you that is." She said not wanting to seem like it was decided even though it obviously had been. They wanted another babysitter. Whatever the reason for their inviting him did not matter to me. I was simply glad he was back.

"Yeah, I figured at least through the end of the summer. See how it is in the fall. Then take it from there kind of thing." Weston said looking over at me as if awaiting my approval.

I smiled. "That would be great." I hugged him again. I could feel Sydney's hand rubbing my back and after a few long moments I allowed the hug to end again. Everyone was smiling now.

"So, what's the plan for the day?" I asked excited for the day for a change.

"I'll go take my stuff up to my room, change, and then let's hit the beach?" Weston asked everyone to see if that sounded good enough.

"Perfect" was all I could say still smiling. It had been the first time in almost 8 weeks that I smiled, and it felt good to do so.

32

"David, what are you doing?" Weston asked me while not looking over but keeping his eyes out towards the ocean.

We all had an amazingly relaxing and perfect day. We got to the beach around noon and by the time we had set up camp it was closing in on 1pm. The girls decided to catch some rays while Kyle, Weston, and I headed out into the ocean. After a couple hours of jumping and swimming in the surf we had made our way back to the blankets and the girls. Kyle stood over Kristi shaking himself off over her like a wet dog might to dry itself off.

"Oh. Hell no! What is your problem?" She sat up angerly. Kyle gave his best grin and said, "Sorry babe." Like that should make it all better.

Weston and I took our spots more respectively than Kyle had, avoiding a big production. Sydney was laying on her back her body exposed to the sun. She really did look great in her dark green bikini and her 2 months of tanning occasionally was quite the accenting feature to her athletic but slim frame.

"Are you hungry? I brought sandwiches." She said without opening her eyes. I got the feeling she knew I was checking her out.

"You know? You really are an amazing person. Still absolutely beautiful as well." I said looking down at her. She turned her head and opened one eye squinting at me. She raised her arm up over her head to shield her eyes from the sun so she could see my face.

"What are you doing?" She asked sheepishly clearly a little embarrassed about my compliment. Clearly, she had not expected me to take notice of her, at least not in a way that expressed some kind of an attraction from me.

"Nothing. I'm just stating the obvious." She rolled her head back to straight again turning away from me.

"Thank you." She said back to me in a soft voice that gave off a hint of embarrassment.

"I'm hungry." Weston stated loud enough for everyone to hear. Sydney sat up and reached into the small cooler we brought and tossed him a sandwich. She then tossed him a cold Bud Light to wash it down with. He took the sandwich from the Ziploc bag and opened it up inspecting it. Sydney noticed him checking out the sandwich and a confused look came over her.

"What are you doing? It's tuna fish" She said to him. She was puzzled over his inspection of the sandwiches she had made for us all.

"I know. I'm just making sure it's actually tuna fish and not something else."

"Something else?" Sydney asked in a curious voice. "What else could it be?"

"Wet cat food. I've seen that done before." He replied. Kyle and I laughed louder than we should have causing other beach goers to look over at us trying to find out what was so funny.

After a few hours of just relaxing, the beach had started to empty out a bit. It was about the time where the tourists start thinking of dinner and evening activities. Locals either eat early or wait until late if they are planning on eating out. No sense in June trying to fight the masses. Once it got to be but just a few others around us we broke out the volleyball and bumped it around for a bit. It turned into a competitive game of trying to get the others to be the reason the ball would hit the sand. Plenty of people got hit, some multiple times, but it was not a mean thing. Quite the opposite really. Kyle would get smacked by Kristi and then we all would laugh. I would hit Weston, Sydney would hit me, and Kyle hit no one since he was the least skilled player in the group. The fun ended when Kristi hit Kyle in the face for the third time. She was obviously aiming for his head which did not make Kyle happy, but it made the rest of us laugh hysterically.

"Now you're going to get it!" Kyle yelled at her as he charged her and carried her off over his shoulder and towards the water.

"No Kyle! No! I still have my clothes on." Kristi said protesting while kicking and screaming the whole way to the water. When he got waist deep, he tossed her as far as he could into the water. When she came up, I was surprised to see her laughing and swimming towards him. I was expecting her to retaliate and was quite surprised when she embraced him a heartfelt kiss instead. It made me smile. Seeing them so in love and so happy together made me a little happier in life.

Weston and I had made our way back to the blankets. Sydney had gone to the water standing calf deep and allowing the water to rush past her, staring out into the ocean she seemed like she too was trying to figure out life's great mysteries. The breeze coming off the ocean made her hair flutter a little exposing her neck a bit. She was stunning to look at.

"David, what are you doing?" Weston asked me not looking over but keeping his eyes out towards the ocean.

I looked at him. "What do you mean?" Confused by his question.

"With her. With Sydney." He replied nodding his head over to Sydney as if giving me directions as to where to look so I could answer his question. I looked back towards the sea and to Sydney.

"She is still so in love with you it's crazy." He added his voice taking a serious tone. I could tell this was going to be an "all joking aside" kind of conversation.

"How do you know that?" I asked him curiously.

"You really are an idiot sometimes." I have heard that a lot I thought to myself.

"The girl rushes to help you after not hearing from you in almost a year. She has not left you since she got here. She isn't working because she is afraid of not being there for you if you need her. She's helped with the housework, doing your laundry and other chores" He emphasized the your part. "She's the one that called me and talked to me about moving back here. Ever wonder where her clothes have come from?" This time he did look over at me. I remained silent since I had no clue.

"She drops you off at work, drives back to Severna Park, gets what she needs and then drives back here to OC. All before needing to pick you up from work so she is there for you."

"I didn't know that" I replied. I was thinking about all he was saying to me. I knew that what Sydney had been doing was obviously a burden on her, I did not know how much of a burden until Weston had provided the insight.

"She hasn't said anything to me about how she feels." I said feeling like the idiot everyone had made me out to be.

"She shouldn't have to. I think her actions speak a lot louder than any words she could say." Weston sounded like he was lobbying for her. Sydney turned back to us and she smiled a small smile, gave a small wave of her hand, then turned back to the water.

"She's been great. She really has. I mean she is great. I just" I paused trying to think of the right words. "I don't know."

"Sarah isn't here David, and it seems that every time you two have issues she runs. And then you both get hurt."

"She'll eventually be back in my life. We always manage to find each other again. I couldn't do that to Syd again." I said.

"Then don't. Next time you and Sarah somehow manage

to find each other do the right thing. Let her go." He stood up still looking out to the water. "In the meantime, love the one that actually loves you."

"You think I can just so easily forget Sarah?" I asked him annoyed that everyone gives that advice and yet has no idea how hard their advice would be to follow.

"No. I'm not asking you to. I'm saying move on. If she's still in your heart, then lock her away for now. Worry about your next encounter with her IF it ever happens. Just don't pass on the good thing standing in front of you for something that may never happen." He started walking towards the water and then turned back to me "Talk to her. Think about it. You at least owe her the conversation." He turned back and ran straight towards Sydney splashing water up onto her perfect form. She screamed not expecting Weston to do that to her. He laughed and dove past her making his way out towards Kyle and Kristi.

Weston was right. I decided I needed to talk to Sydney. I stood up, took a deep breath, and walked slowly up beside her. I could see she had a serious look in her eyes, as if she were bearing the weight of the world upon her. Part of me believed she was dreading this conversation as well, I was not dreading it, but more looking forward to it now that Weston had kind of shed some light onto the whole thing. When I got next to her, I leaned into her nudging her a bit. She smiled but did not look over at me. I got the feeling she did not want to look at me if I was going to break her heart.

"Hi" I said in a soft voice.

"Hey" she replied in just as soft of a voice.

"I'm sorry." I said to her. Now she looked over at me as if confused.

"For what?"

I turned and looked into her eyes so she would know I was being sincere. "For being an ass and for not thanking you sooner for everything you have done over the last couple of months." She turned her eyes back to the ocean. I could tell by her reaction I had caught her off guard and she was not expecting me to thank her. "Thank you, Sydney. Thank you for being here. Thank you for cooking and helping around the house. Thank you for driving me to work, and for making sure I didn't off myself overnight. Thank you for sneaking home to get stuff that you would need so that you'd be back in time to be with me. Thank you for never saying anything when you knew I couldn't talk, and thanks for holding me when I needed it. Thanks for everything that you've done, and that you are doing that I have no idea about. Thank you for being so sweet to me."

She thought about my words for a few moments and then finally gave a simple "You're welcome" I wrapped my arm around her and puller her into a side hug kissing the top of her head.

"Do you know why I am here?" She asked into my chest.

"Yeah. I know why. Your actions say why." I left out that Weston had pointed the obvious out to me.

"And?" She asked. Her voice was both hopeful and fearful at the same time.

"And I'm really happy that you are here. I don't want you to leave. I can't imagine you not being here. Syd, I like you a lot. I've always liked you a lot."

"But you don't love me." She said holding me tighter thinking that the tighter hold would spare her heart some pain.

"I didn't say that!" I said releasing the hug and moving in front of her so I could look at her.

"Then what are you saying?" She asked a little confused as tears formed in her eyes.

"I'm saying I'm a wreck right now. That I couldn't be the guy that you deserve right now. I'm a flipping mess!" I said, my voice rising with every word. I paused for a moment until I knew I could speak without getting so intense "But I am really glad you're here and I'd like you to stay. With me. And maybe I can grow into the kind of guy you deserve?" The last part came out sounding like a question.

She stood straighter leaving the embrace. She was thinking about what I was saying. "I know you're hurting, and no one knows better than I do that you need to get your crap together. That being said, my life is better with you in it David. I'd like to stay and help you still. If you'd have me that is." I pulled her back into a long hug giving her my answer thinking about how much I do not deserve her.

33

"You never told me." I said to Weston after the laughter had died down from Eric's trash talking about how he could hang with us in Go Karting. Eric and his friend Brad had come down for the weekend and had mentioned wanting to do the slick track with my group of friends. I tried to explain that it was not the same go kart experience as the track back in Crofton, but he swore up and down he could hang and "Teach us all a lesson". He had no idea just how good we were. We were ruthless. We would roll in with a group of ten and intentionally get kicked out by constantly ignoring the no bumping rule. The best tactic was to pair up, the lead car would get position on another car, spin them out, and then the trailing partner would lay the hit on the spun-out car at full speed. It was nothing less than brutal, but another way of striking a blow to the tourists in our town. Eric had no idea what he and Brad would be in for.

"Told you what?" Weston answered back unaware of what I was referring to.

"What happened to the girl in Austin? Why would you leave her to come back and babysit me?" I know Weston and I are close friends, the type of friendship that lasts a lifetime, but to leave the girl you love and move back just to babysit seemed a little over the top to me. Especially since it had been two months since the last attempt by me at that point and there were three others with me already.

"Tracy? Was that her name?" Eric asked the group.

"I'll just refer to her forevermore as the slut known as Mustang Sally." Weston replied sipping his beer.

"Wait what?" I asked in shock. "She went after a guy with a Mustang too?" I asked him wanting him to clarify. If that were the case it would be the second girl he had dated that left him for a guy that drove a Mustang.

"Yep. Forget that whore." He replied in a tone that said it was time to change the subject. I could tell he had no interest of rehashing the details of his failed relationship. "Let's get back to the issue at hand and Eric's need for pain. Why would you want to subject yourself to that torture of Go Karting against David and his friends here? I don't even go with them and they consider me part of the group."

"Why don't you go?" Brad asked curiously.

"Because if there aren't enough tourists to go around, they turn on each other, and that gets ugly quick." Weston replied drawing the last part out. "Burn marks from hits causing their bodies to come into contact with the engine, whiplash, bruises from the seatbelt restraining them are just a few of the injuries. Hell, one guy had to drop out of a volleyball tournament because he still couldn't turn his head to the left after a week from being hit. Screw that mess."

Eric and Brad sat silently for a moment and then both said they still wanted to try it and that they thought they could hang. Weston's and my laughter were cut off when Kyle ran out through the back sliding glass door in hysterics.

"Oh shit. Oh shit. Oh shit! I'm dead. I'm dead. She's going to kill me." He was yelling frantically while pacing back and forth in front of us.

"Why is she going to kill you? What did you do this time?" Weston asked. I kind of had a feeling what he was going to say, or at least with whom.

Still, he paced. "So, there's this girl where I work."

"You mean at M.R's?" I asked.

"Yes. Tina. Well, she and I went out after work for a bit" He started to look around wondering if it was just the guys.

"It's safe. They had a girl's night. They'll both be back around 1am." I said letting him know he was free to speak and that everyone here would keep his secret.

"Ok cool. What time is it?" He asked still a little concerned about getting caught in whatever it is he had done.

"Almost midnight" Brad answered.

"Shit. Have to make this quick then before I leave for the night." He replied.

"Just tell us what happened already!" I said starting to get irritated.

"Tina and I went out."

"You said that already" Weston interrupted.

"Anyways, we had a couple of drinks and she kissed me."

"Jesus Kyle." I moaned. I was not liking the direction his story was going.

"That's not it. We went for a drive out near Berlin where she lives, and we grabbed a blanket from my truck and went into a cornfield for some privacy." I closed my eyes picturing the scene. I have met Tina before when I have gone into the store Kyle worked at. She's an attractive girl, young though at 18 compared to him, and I mean just turned 18. She graduated just this last June from Highschool. She was a 5'2 blonde with blue eyes. A small waist but huge boobs to compliment her. She had told him that she had only ever been intimate with one guy and only one time, so I always had the feeling her "innocence" was an attractive quality to him as well.

"And?" Eric asked wanting him to keep going with his story.

"And so, we laid the blanket down and started making out. Next thing I knew we were ripping each other's close off. I mean it was animalistic aggression happening." Brad's mouth hung open mesmerized by Kyle's story. Weston and I were less impressed as this seemed like an average story for him so far. "So, we finally get to it and I mean it was hard, and fast, and so raw. It was amazing. Maybe the best sex I've ever had." Kyle was into the retelling of the events. Even going so far as to act out different things they had done.

"You're running short on time." I reminded him. I was not liking the story since it meant he was cheating on arguably my best friend and my voice showed it.

"Right. Good call. So, we finished together like perfectly at the same time."

"Bullshit" Weston muttered not believing the last part Kyle told us.

"And then we collapsed together, me still laying on top of her, and stayed like that for about 15 minutes. We were just so lost in each other, in the moment." He seemed like he was reliving the moment all over again. He was lost in his memory of the evening.

I broke him out of his thoughts. "So besides cheating on one of my best friends you dick, why else would you be in trouble?" I asked heatedly.

"We walked back to my truck."

"Amigo. Not a truck." Eric broke in reminding him that he drove a toy. At least to us he did.

"Suck it, Eric. You and that Spiffy Neon you drive have no room to talk." Kyle said back in defense of his vehicle. It is true. Eric had no room to talk. He drove a Dodge Sporty Neon. We all laughed since it literally said "Sporty" on it like that somehow helped overcome the fact that it was still a Neon. The rest of our group always referred to it as a "Spiffy Neon" because the fact that it was a Sporty Neon did not actually make it sportier looking, just more expensive. At least in our opinions.

"Anyways" he said exaggerating the whole word making

it last a good 5 seconds to say. "When we got back, I started to really itch all over my back and my ass and the back of my legs. Then I noticed why." He seemed worried again now that he had arrived at the end of his story.

"Why?" I asked suspiciously.

"Look!" He yelled turning his back to us and lifting his shirt. His back was covered with what looked like a thousand mosquito bites and the bites had definitely left their mark. Huge bumps covered his back. There was not an area on him that was not covered.

"My ass and legs look just as bad as my back!" He yelled. The four of us could not contain ourselves any longer understanding his plight and the back deck erupted into laughter.

"Oh sure. Laugh it up." We did and every time he talked; we could not help but start up again.

"What am I going to do? Kristi will come home and want me like she always does, and she'll feel this and ask me what happened. How the hell do I explain this to her?" The laughter continued.

"I'm serious! What do I do? It's almost 1am. I need to go." He was worried. I decided to help him.

"Look, go home. I'll tell her you had to go home unexpectedly and that you would call her in the morning. Make something up. Grandma was in the hospital, Dad needed your help with something, mom's car died, something. Then come back tomorrow evening. If you put stuff on it tonight before you leave and all-day tomorrow those bites will be gone by the time you get back tomorrow night."

"Yeah. That should be good. Ok I'll see you guys tomorrow night."

He headed back inside so he could leave right away before he got through the door, I continued my thought "And don't ever make me lie to Kristi again. You be straight with her." He nodded and continued through the door.

"What and idiot. Has he never done it at night outside before?" Weston asked the group. The rest of us just laughed at his unfortunate end to an otherwise great evening.

34

Kyle had taken our advice and had gone home for the evening. No one knew the excuse he had provided Kristi and thank God; she did not ask us about it. I was not sure I had it in me to lie to her even if she had asked.

Kyle did manage to make it home by 6pm the next evening and we made plans to take Eric and Brad to the track. No matter how hard anyone had lobbied against the idea they still wanted to go believing they had what it took to compete. How stupid were they?

It was an unusually quiet evening at the Go Kart track, so we took full advantage of it. We raced hard, and violently. Brad did not make it around one single lap and poor Eric got hit so hard at the end that his glasses flew off his face and his watch came off his wrist. The track attendant had to stop the ride for Eric to pick up his stuff. In the end both Brad and Eric went home rubbing their sore necks and complaining about how much money they had spent without enjoying themselves. Both vowed to never go to the track with us again.

The next day had another misadventure with Eric filleting himself with my surfboard. For some reason he decided to hop off the board when an approaching wave had crested in front of him. Instead of diving under it he jumped off and pulled the board next to him. The force of the wave ripped the board away from his grip, but not without the skegs going across his belly. He looked like someone took a filet knife from one side to the other just above his belly button. The gash did not bleed all that much, but enough for us to force him out of the water before attracting any unwanted predators. Eric had mentioned that evening that it stung a little but otherwise he had thought that he would survive. That was the last time Eric ever went surfing with us.

35

Sydney and I decided to make a trip back to the Annapolis area. She was wanting to get some more of her things, and I felt the need to check in with my parents as well. It was the last weekend of August and still on the hot side as far as the outside temperatures were concerned. Once I dropped her off at her house, I figured I would stop by the pier Kyle and I would crab from. It was so peaceful there and although I did not need the peace and serenity for my current mental health, I still loved the view and the quiet the spot offered.

Once parked I made my way out to the edge of the pier not noticing that someone else was there as well. I was lost in thought of how good things were going with Sydney, how loving she had always been, and her green eyes when a voice brought me back from my thoughts.

"Hey David." A sullen voice spoke to me. I turned my eyes away from the water to make sure the voice was from who I thought had spoken. I was surprised to see Sarah there. She did not look happy, but rather sad, depressed, lonely even. Seeing her upset was always a weakness of mine and my heart would instantly break when I knew she was sad.

"Sarah. What's wrong? Is everything ok?" I asked taking a seat next to her. She shook her head no and her silent sobs renewed. I pulled her close in a side long hug and tried to console her as best as I could. "Shhh. Be still now. I am here for you." Hearing my words, and the words I chose, she clung to me tighter as if I were a life preserver keeping her afloat in whatever sea of torment she was currently swimming through. I allowed her to, I did not speak but chose to remain silent as well, and when her embrace on me loosened I let that happen too.

She sat up a little straighter but chose to still lean up against me. She took my free hand in-between both of hers and stared out into the river. "Guys are jerks." She choked out then wiped a tear from her cheek. I chose not to respond. She laughed a little at my silence. "It's ok. You can speak David."

"What would you like me to say?"

Another tear fell. "You could agree with me." I did, I knew what I was like to her, or could be when lost in my selfishness, but I did not vocalize it to her.

"Did you want to talk about it?" I asked then pulled her closer with the arm still wrapped around her.

"No. Not really." She managed to get out returning the tighter hold. "What are you doing here?" She asked me as if remembering I do not live in the area any longer. It must have been a little surprising to see me at the pier. Then again, I always considered this my pier since it was my friends Romonzo and Beth that had shown me this place. I was kind enough to share it with Sarah one night after a date she and I had, and I guess she did not lie when she told me how peaceful it seemed here to her. The same thought I had of the place. Now, end of August, still a warm summer evening, looking out across the still water and occasionally watching a fish catch and insect floating on the surface, my thoughts of this place were reconfirmed. It is peaceful.

"I came back to visit my family for the weekend. I love this place. I try to stop by whenever I am here in the area. I told you, it's peaceful to me here." I left out the part about Sydney being in town as well.

She gripped my hand tighter. "Thank you." She whispered.

"Sarah. I have not done anything worth thanking me for."

"You are here. Holding me. Holding my hand. That is exactly what I need right now." I said nothing, but the wooden bench we were sitting on was causing me to get a little stiff as I was trying not to move since I thought Sarah seemed comfortable. I finally had to as my leg was falling asleep. "Please don't go yet." She whispered to me.

"I won't leave you. Not until you are ready."

She looked up to me "Do you have a blanket? Can we lay on the beach for a bit?" Her voice was still soft and hurt sounding, and I knew I could not resist her request. I stood up and pulled her up as well so that we could continue holding hands and then walked with her back to my car. I grabbed the blankets from my trunk and lead her back to the little beach near the pier. I set the blanket down and she laid down on her side pulling me down next to her but in a way so that we were facing each other. She still clung to my hand as if it were the most valuable thing in the world to her now. I still did not speak, allowing her a chance to enjoy the silence a bit.

I had not noticed when it had turned dark, but it had. I had arrived around 5pm so I figured it must be around 9pm now. I chose not to check my watch thinking that might seem rude.

"You have somewhere you need to be?" She asked as if knowing my thoughts. She knew, she always knew my concerns and thoughts. I looked into her perfectly blue eyes and felt immediately lost in them.

"No Sarah. I am here for as long as you want me to be." She rolled over to her other side turning away from me but pulled me closer to her so that we were spooning. She laid her head on my hand that she kept in a firm grip between hers as well.

"Good. I am glad to hear that. I may let you leave in the morning."

I could tell her mood was lifting. The tears were no longer flowing from her eyes and a small smile had found its way onto her face. I did not move or speak for fear of breaking the moment. I waited for Sarah to take the lead and see where this interaction would go. Eventually she released her grip of my hand, rolled on to her back freeing my arm that had fallen asleep under her, and propped herself up on her elbows looking out to the river.

"This is such a beautiful little spot. Thank you, David, for showing it to me."

I flipped over as well allowing the blood back into my arm. "You're welcome." She turned her head too me and I could see a sly smile form on her face as if a thought had entered her mind.

"Do you bring all your girls here?" She asked still smiling. I turned to look at her so she could see I was telling the truth.

"Sarah, I never take any girls to any of our spots or places we have been to. I feel like they are our places, our memories, and I would not share those with another."

"So, you've never taken Sydney to The Narrows, or here, or the lake?" She asked testing me. She turned back away from me and faced the water again. "God, you better not have taken her to our lake."

This made me smile. The fact that she considered it our lake when it was a two-minute walk from my parent's house amused me. I felt the same way of course, but it made it some-how more special knowing she felt the same.

"No Sarah. I have never taken anyone to places you and I would go. Never." It was true, I have never been able to take Syd anywhere I went with Sarah. Why would I? "Sarah, the beach is a little different. I mean I don't take her to things you and I would frequent, but obviously there are things that Sydney and I do that you and I would before as well."

"Like what?" She asked curiously.

"Oh, I don't know. Mini golf comes to mind. We go every now and then." That was a minor thing I thought but thought to add "but never to the courses you and I would go to."

"And? Anything else?" She asked still bearing her sly smile. She was clearly amused with her little testing of me.

"Come on Sarah. That is not fair. She lives with me. Obviously, we walk the beach, do the boardwalk, go out to eat, and other stuff that people who are together would do. That does not mean though that I take her to the same places that I would take you or share the same kind of intimacy with her that you and I did." I felt like that came out a little raw so I figured I would try to reassure her again. "Certain things though are ours. The Narrows, the lake, here, the Fun House, making love on the beach, even Wild World to me is special, and I will never share those places or experiences with another."

She laid back down and turned to face me once more, so I did the same. There we were lying on the blanket, underneath the stars, by the water, and completely unaware of anything else but each other. "I still love you. You know that don't you?" She said looking into my eyes.

"I don't know Sarah. Yes, part of me believes that you do, but part of me realizes it doesn't matter." I rolled over onto my back looking up to the night sky.

"Doesn't matter?" She asked curiously.

"Look Sarah, I will always love you, and you say you feel the same, but the reality is that's not enough for you. I have never been enough for you. I really wish I could have been, but it doesn't seem to matter how much you say you love me, you always find a reason to leave. Maybe it has been my fault, but some of the stuff, to me at least, is so minor and could have been worked out. Anyways, I feel like I am not enough for you. I have always felt that way, I have always felt you were way to good for me, so I am not sure what to think anymore. I don't know, I am not communicating this very well I don't think. Bottom line is that I am not enough, the fact that you love me, and I love you is not enough for you to be happy." Now I had tears filling my eyes.

I could not tell her everything. I could not tell her how I think she runs at the first sign of me needing something from her, like understanding, or grace, no, there is now way I could tell her that. Confessing that I feel like I have never been enough for her was hard enough.

"David, I'm not sure what to say to that." Sarah replied as if not understanding the thoughts I shared. I could tell she did not agree with them either.

"You don't have to say anything Sarah. It's how I feel. If you think I am wrong then show me, but don't tell me." There was sadness in my voice and maybe a hint of anger as well.

Sarah moved closer to me and wrapped my arm underneath her once more. She laid her head on my chest and we sat there for the rest of the night in silence. When the dawn broke and we watched as the sun reflected off the river, it was then that she decided to continue our conversation.

"Can I see again? Are you in town for the whole weekend?" She asked in a groggy voice. Neither one of us slept much, maybe only catching a few winks here and there.

"I don't know Sarah. I'd like too, but I am not sure this weekend it will be possible." She stared at me for a long while.

"She's here too, isn't she?" She asked clutching my hand tighter.

"Yes. Sydney is here too. She came back with me." She let go of my hand and hugged me tight after hearing this. My heart ached for her, but for the first time my heart was guarded from her. I needed more than a few hours of her free time and some hand holding to go down this road again. I kissed the top of her head. "Look Sarah, I'll be staying at my parent's, call me there. Maybe we can hang out for a bit." I rolled over on my side so I could see her "I need to go though. I have other things planned for the day." She leaned over and kissed me softly then stood pulling me up along with her.

"I leave for Frostburg next week. Any chance you would come out and visit me?"

I knew I would make that happen, as did she. "I'd like that. I'll need your phone number so I can call you." I was excited at the idea of visiting her in Frostburg.

"I don't have it yet. Once I get there and get settled in, I will call you and we can work out a date. Hopefully, mid-September?" She too was starting to sound a little excited.

We had made the walk back to our cars and we were standing next to hers as I leaned in and kissed her goodbye. I opened her car door for her so she could get in.

"So, two weeks? I'll hear from you in two weeks?" I asked her for clarification. She smiled at my enthusiasm.

"At the latest. Two weeks." She stood up and kissed me again. "And David?"

"Yes Sarah?"

She sat back down in the driver's seat and pulled the door closed then rolled down her window so she could finish her thought. "It's not goodbye. It's good morning." She laughed as she backed the car out and sped up the hill away from our little spot. I waived as she honked the horn on her way out wondering if she would indeed call as well as wondering what had made her so upset.

36

October was soon upon us. My trip to Frostburg did not happen, at least not yet. In fact, the phone call from Sarah never came where she was supposed to give me the info of where she was living, or how to contact her, and to be honest the more time that past the less I remembered that she was supposed to call. Eventually I forgot all about my supposed trip to see her. To me it was more evidence of not being enough for her. A sad thought really, I am not enough, and yet if she were to need anything I would do my best to fulfill those needs.

The weather was changing with the days staying warm, but the nights were starting to get cool. You could feel it in the weather and see it all around in nature. Trees seemed less lively. Plants were no longer sending up new flowers and the older ones were starting to wither. Sydney and I though were flourishing. We shared thoughts and feelings. We shared meals and time together. We walked the beaches, went to the boardwalk, held hands when we wanted, and kissed when it felt right. We shared a room and a bed, but we were not intimate in a sexual way. It was not that I did not want to or that she did not want to, but rather an unspoken agreement to wait until the time was right.

Both of us were feeling out the other trying to gauge if the other was ready. It was nice, the not going too fast but keeping it slow and steady kind of thing. Neither one of us ever pressured the other. As we were growing closer though, Kyle and Kristi were fading away. It was sad to watch. An ending of something that seemed so real. Who was I to judge? I thought Sarah and I would be together forever and that does not quite ring true anymore. Kyle had been taken in by the slut from M.R.'s. She had cast her spell upon him, and he had fallen willingly.

There was no huge fight for Kyle and Kristi. No discussion about the relationship. No breakup to get over. Just a simple fading away of the relationship. I do not know if Kristi ever knew about the teen aged blonde chick from his work or not, and she never said one way or the other, she just simply said she was moving home one day and knew that her days at the beach were over.

By the end of October, she had met a midshipman from the Naval Academy and had once again fallen in love. I was happy for her, but sad in knowing that living with two of my best friends was over and looking back on the good times we shared always brought a tear to my eye.

Kyle still lived at the beach. Choosing to commute back and forth to school. Weston had decided to stay as well opting to carpool with Kyle. Sydney decided to stay with me full time. She was ever so faithful and one Friday evening in October after a perfect evening at home alone cooking together and enjoying a movie on cable "it" finally happened.

It was not awkward at all, in fact it felt really right to be with her and though it had been well over a year since the last time we had enjoyed each other's company in that way it seemed as if both of us remembered exactly what the other wanted. That evening I believe Sydney had finally made it past the ghost of Sarah Fulton.

We were still laying on the floor by the fireplace when Kyle had rushed through the front door in a panic. Kyle had been bowling in a local PBA regional event and I was not expecting him back so early. Kyle never looked at us or even acknowledged that we were there but rather dashed straight up to his room and slammed the door behind him. Weston came in roughly two minutes behind him only he chose to come into the living room. He took in the scene, processed what it meant, and then smiled. I could tell he was not going to let this pass without causing a little embarrassment.

"Well alright" He said dragging out alright. "Now this is what I'm talking about!" Sydney buried her face into the blanket.

"Weston! Quit!" I said trying to get him to stop.

"It's about time you two really got back together." He looked up the stairs as if another thought occurred to him. We could hear Kyle speaking into the phone.

"But you said you would be there!" He almost yelled but it came out as more of a whine.

"Can you pass me her sweats please?" I asked Weston. Not taking his eyes off the hallway upstairs as he gently tossed Sydney her clothes. She hurriedly went about the task of getting dressed.

"Weren't they supposed to be gone for a while yet?" She asks somewhat irritated yet mixed with embarrassment.

"That's what they said." I watched her finish throwing on the sweats and my sweatshirt and grab the rest of her clothes. "God you're gorgeous" I said to her.

She looked down at me and smiled then kissed the top of my head. "I love you." She said after the kiss. She started hurrying to pick up a bit in an attempt to erase the evidence of the evening. I stayed on the floor still covered by only the blanket we had been using.

"I love you too." I said back to her using as serious of a tone as I could so that she knew I was telling the truth. She stopped what she was doing and looked over at me.

"I do." I was looking right into her eyes "I want you to know and to believe me." She held my gaze for a long moment then dropped the clothes of ours she was holding and ran over to me and sat on my lap embracing me in a long hard hug. After a few moments of rocking her, she whispered "Thank you" to me.

"No Sydney, thank you. You've done so much for me and

have never asked anything of me. Thank you for loving me." I said back to her. She tightened the hug and I reciprocated.

"But you said you would be there!" Kyle had yelled once again. Sydney and I separated and looked up at the ceiling.

"What's going on?" I asked Weston who was still staring up the stairs. He sighed and took a seat on the couch. Once seated he started to explain.

"You know the girl with the golden vagina?" He asked. Sydney and I shook our heads that we knew who he was talking about. That had become her new nickname once Kyle and Kristi had faded away. Since everyone knew that Kristi was the best girlfriend he had ever had we figured the M.R. slut must have had a golden vagina in order to get him to give up on something so good as Kristi and the nickname kind of stuck.

"Well since this tournament was so close, she told him that she would be there. She never showed up and he was frazzled the whole event. He bowled like shit and kind of blames her. Once he was done and pretty much eliminated, we raced home so he could find out what happened to her. He was worried that she may have been in an accident or something. I assumed she just didn't want to come." He looked back at the ceiling and then continued "Sounds like I was right."

"Fuck you then!" We heard Kyle yell from upstairs. A few silent minutes later Kyle made his way down the stairs and stood facing us. He looked a little sullen.

"I was used. Fucked and chucked." Sydney, Weston and I looked at each other wondering what the hell he was talking about.

"You're going to have to explain better than that." I finally said.

"She used me. She was supposed to come today and didn't. When I asked her why she said she didn't feel like it. I asked why she didn't call to let me know and she said why should she have to do that? It's not like we are together or anything." The looks back and forth started again.

"Not together?" Sydney asked.

"Yeah. She said we went out, had a few laughs, and that was it. She didn't want anything serious and if I couldn't handle that then I need to move on." Sydney laughed. Then I laughed. Finally, Weston did too.

"I know right?" Kyle said. "She says we can still have sex every now and then, but she doesn't want to be my girlfriend and she isn't even sold on dating. Just sex occasionally if she feels like it." He added perplexed by it all. We started laughing again.

"I'm being used for sex. I told her I wasn't a piece of meat and I wasn't doing that. To take all of me or nothing."

"And?" Sydney asked knowing the answer.

"She said ok bye then and told me she can find someone else willing to do her." He shook his head. "What the fuck is wrong with chicks?" We all laughed again while the irony totally escaped our friend, the resident man whore back in the day, Kyle. We all stopped laughing when he asked a serious question.

"I can't believe I let Kristi go. Do you think there is any chance I can save things with her?" His voice was both regretful and mournful as if the realization of what he had lost finally hit him. I answered as gently as I could figuring it was my place to do so.

"No Kyle. That ship has sailed. I'm sorry, but Kristi is gone for good." He thought about my words for a while as we all stayed silent to let him think.

He shook his head as if the finality of it sunk in and he muttered one word as he made his way up the stairs. "Damn."

37

It was a strange thing to see to say the least, Kyle moping around over a girl, or two, was not something I was used to seeing. I was not sure exactly how to handle it. I had been the one requiring help for the last couple of years and I had completely forgotten how to look after others. The need to make him happy was still there, but the memory of accomplishing this for others somehow escaped me.

Where Kyle had struck out with the fairer sex Weston seemed to be thriving. He had met a tall brunette with blue eyes named Molly.

"Best thing about her is I know I've got her for a while." He said to us one night confidently.

"Why's that?" Sydney had asked him curious as to why Weston of all people would feel so confident.

"She's into Jags, not Mustangs. Ain't no guy our age driving around in a Jag so unless she plans on finding someone way older, I should be good for a couple of years."

That brought a smile to Kyle's face which in turn made the rest of us laugh as well. I felt quite confident that Kyle would eventually find love again. And if not love at the very least lust. Sometimes, when he was down on weekends, he would ask Weston or myself if we would go out with him to chat up girls with him. Just to be a wingman.

"I need you David! No one is better at carrying a conversation better than you." He would beg of me. It was true, I guess. Back in the day he would be great at the opening lines and I would do the rest with him chiming in here and there. That shitty smile of his and an opening line as simple as "God your beautiful" was enough to capture their interests 90% of the time. I would politely decline and suggest Weston instead.

"Are you joking? You know how he is with the ladies" He would respond in irritation thinking it was a ridiculous suggestion.

"Hey, he's gotten better apparently. That self-deprecating crap seems to work. Maybe you should try that." I would suggest while he would shake his head and walk away not happy at my unwillingness to tag along.

"Was I really that bad?" Weston would ask. "I mean I always got mine if you know what I mean."

I would just stare at him then answer "In High School you thought it appropriate to grab ass and slam your tongue down their throat no matter what. Even if it was just a "friends" date. Then brag to us about how "She had a great ass". Definitely not smooth." I told him emphasizing the great ass part. He was a clown when it came to dating or even talking to a girl back then.

"Like I said. I got mine" He said smiling while defending his ability to woo the fairer sex.

Honestly, the real reason I did not want to do it was because I did not want to make waves with Syd. I had done that once with Kyle before, the day after prom when I was with Sarah to be exact, what I thought was something innocent ended up not going so well later, as Jen, aka The Whore from Dundalk, thought there was more to it than what it was and, on several occasions, it had gone way too far.

Sydney would say it would be fine with her if I did and just kept it to talking and only for Kyle's benefit if I wanted to. Truth is I did not trust myself. Why tempt the demons? The rust from being in a long-term relationship did not last long and soon there was a parade of weekend long guests that Kyle would bring home. I could not keep up with the different names. He would joke with us about how he wanted to sleep the alphabet. Meaning have sex with girls where their names started with a different letter of the alphabet. He thought Q would be tough but that he could do it. I believed he could thinking X might be just too hard. He may have to settle for a name with an X in it instead.

Weston and Molly though were moving along nicely. She was a nice girl. Patient as Job and a heart that was huge. I could tell she really cared for Weston. He seemed to generally care for her as well. Weston was himself and somehow that was ok with her. She played along with his full speed ahead antics and somehow still managed to fall for him. As I have said before, to each his Dulcinea. Weston was hers. It did not bother any of us that she would stay every weekend. She got along with everyone and Sydney would take her out sometimes in the afternoons for some girl time. Shopping and stuff. Whatever girls do. They always seemed so happy when they got home, and it seemed to brighten up the house when they would return home.

Thankfully though they did not frequent the antique places that Kristi was in to. No more hideous looking lamps, or umbrella holders, nothing that made the place junkier looking. Ironically, the pig umbrella holder and matching lamp stayed. I was willing to get rid of it wanting to be rid of anything that Sarah had brought into the house, but Sydney liked it and wanted it to stay. The thought occurred to me that she wanted to keep it around as a reminder to me of what had happened so that if the opportunity ever came to talk or see her again, I might remember what always seems to happen. If that was her secret plan, I think it worked. As I know that my heart will forever hold a spot for Sarah because I know that I will always love her, so too do I know that I will always resent her a little as well.

Sydney and I grew as close as two people could be, I think. Loving Sunday night through Friday mornings and then just trying to make it through the weekend with everyone around. It is not that we hated the weekends, it was just somehow.......

less. Our alone time together was great. Quiet. Peaceful. Intimate. Alone with each other and appreciating the time we had together.

Halloween and Thanksgiving flew by. I have always loved Halloween and liked to get as many of the group together as I could. This year was no different with 30 of us hitting a haunted hayride in Columbia. It was a great time, and we all had a blast. Not much going on around the beach at that time so it is always up to me to have to travel if I want the spooks and scares for entertainment.

Thanksgiving was spent with Sydney's family. Her parents were not exactly warm and fuzzy towards me, but who could blame them? I am sure they felt like Sydney was wasting her time living at the beach. I understood and I did not hold it against them either. Part of me often wondered if maybe I was wasting my life living here, but I could not help myself. I loved it here. I still felt as if this is where I needed to be at this moment in time.

Christmas though seemed special this year. I had never felt closer to Sydney. Sure, it was not the same as with Sarah, but would anyone ever be? I can still hear Weston's words to me "love the one that actually loves you." And without realizing it, I had. I knew what I needed to do. What I wanted to do! And on Christmas day, as we were spending it alone in our little house at the beach, enjoying a fire and some adult style eggnog, I presented her with her last gift that I had gotten her.

I saved it for last hoping she would love it. Not that she would not appreciate the clothes I had gotten her, or the gift certificate to her favorite restaurant back home, or the CD's, but because this one would mean more to her than all those combined. She could not take her eyes off the little box waiting to be opened. Syd knew it was some kind of jewelry but did not know what to expect, and when she finally opened the box and saw the gold ring with a heart in the middle of it and a tiny little diamond in the center of the heart her eyes went big.

"David, is this what I think it is?" She asked me in an unsteady voice not quite sure what to make of the ring.

"Possibly" I answered back. Her eyes teared up a little. "Sydney, what I am asking is, well it's like this, I am still somewhat of a little bit of a show as you know. I need to get my crap straight. I am asking you if you would wear this as a promise ring? Until I get my crap taken care of and can properly ask you to spend the rest of your life with me kind of thing. The guy at the store swore there was such a thing as a promise ring." I said a little unsure of what I was asking.

She thought about it for a moment. "It's beautiful." Then she looked at me "You are asking me to wait until you get your ducks in a row? And that you do want to marry me in the future?" I nodded. That sounded like what I was fumbling around saying. A smile grew on her face and she lunged into my arms and lap. She felt so good as she hugged me tightly. She was wearing her red leggings and my white Endless Summer sweatshirt and a Santa hat. She felt warm to hug as her body seemed to radiate happiness in that moment.

"I will wear this ring proudly David! I will happily wait for you." I hugged her back as tightly as I could never wanting to let her go. At that moment I was in about as perfect of a moment as I had experienced in a long, long time. The rest of the day I knew would be just as perfect.

38

"Let's hit some golf balls" Brent suggested from the back seat of my car.

It was a cold night in February. A Tuesday night to be exact. Bowling night. I had made the drive from the beach earlier in the afternoon which was my normal Tuesday routine in order to bowl in this league I loved back in Crofton. Kyle bowled in it as well as Brent. Brent was a couple of years younger than I was but was one of the guys that had grown up in the bowling leagues as well. He had dark hair and eyes and when he smiled his eyes would squint making him look kind of like a rodent.

He had a great sense of humor, one of those kinds of people that could make you laugh just by laughing himself and he was quick with his wit. He fit in well with the rest of the bowling group. His most well-known feature though had to be his size. Although he was average height, maybe 5'10 or so, it was his weight that made him so large. Brent had to be close to a slim 292 pounds.

The drinks had been flowing steadily, and although it was after 11pm, I was not ready to make the drive back to the beach.

"Golf balls?" Kyle asked from the passenger seat of my car.

"We could hit up Nighthawk?" Weston said in a questioning tone. Weston had chosen to make the trip with me allowing

Sydney some quality alone time back at the beach.

"Now that's an idea. Let's fill up the backpacks and go to a field somewhere to round them off." I had proposed to the group. All seemed to like the idea and we made our way to the local driving range known as Nighthawk.

The moon was full and provided plenty of light for us to see. I parked my car in the median near a pottery business that was located across the street from the driving range. We grabbed the two backpacks and hopped the fence to the driving range. Within 30 minutes we had both packs filled and made our way back to the car. Brent noticed the par 3 course off to the side and eyed the flagstick closest to us.

"I've always wanted a flagstick. I think I'm going to grab one." He dropped the pack he was carrying and made his way to the closest stick. Kyle and I looked at each other smiling widely before turning and heading off to the course to get our own sticks much to the displeasure of Weston.

"Guys! This is taking too much time!" We could hear him yelling to us. A short 5 minutes later the three of us were back with Weston each carrying our own flagstick. Mine was the number 2.

Weston shook his head. "Can we go now please?"

We made our way back to the car and without any kind of an issue. We decided to head back to the bowling and alley where there was some open space to hit from and hit towards the new 7 story office building that was in the early stages of construction. We had hit the two backpacks worth of balls and had driven back by the building retrieving as many as we could. We had found enough to fill one of the packs.

It was fun! Every time a ball clanked off the building it made us all laugh. When we had driven back to the field, we had decided to be on the side closest to the bowling alley parking lot so that when we were done, we could all head our separate ways.

We were still laughing when we saw a police car make the turn at the light to head our way. Kyle rounded one more off.

"Oh shit." I said a little nervous.

"We're fine" Brent offered trying to seem somewhat confident. It was then that 4 other cop cars pulled in surrounding my car.

"No. We're fucked" I said seeing the cops all pull up.

"Put your hands where I can see them!" We were ordered by one of the five officers standing in front of us. We did what was asked of us and stood in a line so that they could see us. Four of the officers began to frisk us checking for weapons or anything else illegal.

"Open you hand" I could hear one of the officers' demand of Kyle. When his fist opened a golf ball fell to the ground bouncing towards the officer and off his left shoe. He bent over and picked the golf ball up examining it closely. I rolled my eyes. Nice Kyle. Nice.

We were asked for our ID's and handed them over. Each of us answering the questions put to us. The only one not talking was Brent.

"Just what the hell are you guys up too? We received a noise complaint." One of the officers said looking at me.

"Well, we were bored so we decided to hit a few golf balls across the street."

The officer looked in the direction I was pointing to. "Bored huh? Do any damage to the building?"

"Not that we know off." I responded confident that we had not.

One of the other officers looked at Brent noticing that he was sweating. "Boy why you sweating?" He asked Brent casually.

"I'm fat" Brent answered flatly. The other officers laughed.

"You don't look fat to me. What are you? Maybe 292lbs?" The officer responded back to Brent.

"I'm fat." He responded for the second time. The laughter started a new.

One of the officers took off in his squad car to check on the building to make sure no damage had occurred while another one was rummaging through the backpacks.

"I'm assuming these aren't your golf balls." The officer said looking up at Weston noticing the standard red line across the middle of the ball in order to say that it was a range ball and not meant for actual play on a course.

"No sir" Weston said while shaking his head. Weston then told him where they came from. It was then that the flagsticks were noticed by the officers.

"Shit boys. Why'd you have to take the flagsticks? If it were just the balls, we could have dumped them over the fence and sent you on your way, but the flags would be noticed. Not like we know where they go." The officer said shaking his head.

"We could show you." Kyle offered up as a solution.

"Too late for that. Now it gets complicated."

A call came over the radio reporting no damage at the construction site and no damage reported at Nighthawk as well. The four of us sighed a little in relief. We could hear another voice on the radio saying the owners wanted to wait until tomorrow to see if they noticed anything before pressing charges, but if not, they would not seek any action against us. Another sigh of relief.

"Well boys, looks like your lucky day. You can go for now." Our tense bodies eased a bit. "If the owners decide to press charges though, well I'm sure you'll end up finding out one way or another." He said smiling. The officers started to disperse to their cars.

"Mind if I grab my club from the bushes?" Kyle asked one of the remaining officers.

"Is it yours? Or one of theirs?" The cop asked back.

"It's mine." Kyle said in response. The officer walked over and picked the club up from the bushes. He examined it for a moment then took a few practice swings as if he were wishing he were somewhere else playing golf.

"Nice swing" Weston commented. I looked down to the ground in disbelief. I just wanted to leave and here Weston is commenting on his swing. The officer, looking close to retirement age, looked over at Weston a little upset at being brought out of his daydream.

"Shut up kid." He said in a disgruntled voice. He tossed the club to Kyle. "Now get the fuck out of here."

We took the que and jumped into my car as fast as we could and left the bowling alley parking lot. When we saw that we were not being followed we decided to park by the lake near my parent's place and relax for a moment.

"Holy shit that could've been bad" Kyle commented first.

"Yeah, a lot worse." Weston added.

"Jesus" was all I could say knowing how close we came to going to jail for a spell. After a long period of silence Brent decided to chime in.

"We didn't do anything wrong." It was the only thing he had said the whole entire time other than "I'm fat".

39

April warmth was upon us and as Sydney and I sat on the back deck soaking up the warmth and sucking down some vodka's and OJ when the thought occurred to me that this was the day a year ago that I had made my last unsuccessful attempt at ending my life. So much had changed in this last year and yet so little as well. I guess it was not the amount of change as much as it was the significance of the changes.

Kristi was gone and oh how I missed my best friend. I missed her perfectly timed humor, or her just as perfectly timed rebukes, either way you could not help but smile when she was around. We still chatted as often as we could and Sydney, God bless her, was great about my continued relationship with Kristi. She now really understood that Kristi was never the threat. She would even walk in if I was on the phone with Kristi, ask who it was, then tell me to say hi to her for her. That is growth.

One of the best changes must be Weston's return. I cannot say enough about how much I love having him around. Molly is ok as well. She is a nice girl who really likes Weston and the two of them seemed to complement each other well.

Then of course there was the biggest change in my life, Sydney. I never would have guessed that a year later Sarah would be out of my life yet again and that I would be promised to another, but that is indeed what has happened. Sydney could not be more perfect for me right now. She looked over at me interrupting my thoughts shielding her eyes from the sun with her hand.

"You're awfully quiet this morning. Whatcha thinking

about over there?" I reached my arm over to her extending my hand to her silently requesting her hand in return. She dropped her hand from her forehead and placed her hand in mine now squinting from the sun as she continued to look over at me waiting for a response.

"I was just thinking how much has changed in the last year." I finally said somewhat cryptically.

"Oh yeah?" She asked a little suspiciously.

"Yeah. I was thinking how much I miss Kristi in the house. Her little one-liners, criticisms, jokes, that kind of thing."

"Oh" She turned her head away from me and closed her eyes from the sun. "Call her. Invite her down."

Now I looked over at her. "You think that would be ok?" I asked in amazement at her suggestion. Sydney has done amazingly with her jealousy of Kristi, but I never would have expected her to suggest inviting her down.

"It's our place too you know. I think Kyle is in an ok place now to handle it. I mean it has been a while since they ended at this point and isn't he on like V in his little alphabet game? I think he would be ok." She laughed a bit "Might motivate him to finish the alphabet this weekend." We both laughed at that thought.

"Ok. I'll go call her." I got up and went inside and dialed Kristi kissing Sydney on the top of her head along the way. Kristi answered on the third ring.

"Hello?" She said in a tired voice.

"Wake up Half Pint. I want you to come to the beach this weekend." I said excitedly into the phone. Half Pint was a nickname I had given her for a couple of reasons. First, and most obvious, was her size. Secondly though, I had always thought she looked a little like Laura Ingles from the TV show Little House on The Prairie, only with darker hair.

"The beach? Will he be there?" She asked me. I paused for a moment not sure if I wanted to tell her the truth or not.

"Yeah. Kyle will be here. As far as I know I mean."

She did not hesitate at all. "Ok. This could be fun." Then she laughed. "I'll shower and head on down."

"Not worried about your classes?" I asked her.

"It's Friday. Screw it. Sydney going to be ok with this?" She asked me. I could not tell if she wanted the extra drama or not.

"It was her idea actually."

"Cool. See you in about three hours." She said before hanging up the phone.

Once Kristi made it into town the three of us headed off to the beach for the day. It was a warmer day getting close to 80 degrees and the sun was at its brightest with no sign of a cloud in the sky. Syd had suggested skipping going to allow Kristi and I to hang out together, but Kristi and I scoffed at the idea and told her she was coming and would like it. I think Syd did not want to feel like a third wheel and so Kristi and I made sure she had no reason to feel like that.

When the two girls felt enough sun rays had been soaked up for the day, we made our way back to the house. I set about to the task of starting dinner, Spaghetti with shrimp and clams as the meat in the sauce. I made enough for six since I knew Weston, Molly and Kyle tried their best to get here by 5pm so we could all eat together. It was kind of an unspoken tradition with us, to eat Friday dinner together.

Kristi and Sydney had started the blender and were planning on making frozen Sex on The Beach drinks as our cocktails for the evening and by the time Weston and Molly had come through the door, we were already on our third drinks and feeling no pain.

"Davey" Weston called out first through the door. I hated when he called me that. "Your first love is home." That made me laugh. A private joke of ours since back in Tenth grade. I do not remember how that got started, or why, but it was something that we said to each other still till this day. Even if I called him back at his parents' house in Gambrills, I would leave a message with his mom saying to just let him know his first love called.

"We have a guest this weekend." Sydney yelled to Weston and Molly from the kitchen turning the blender on as she did. Weston and Molly made their way into the kitchen and their eyes went wide seeing Kristi.

"Drinks?" Kristi said handing both a glass filled with the tasty concoction.

It was evident in my little 5'2 friend that the alcohol was kicking in as she had that glazed over look in her eyes. Weston laughed, took the drink, and gave her a quick hug. Molly waved and said hi forgoing the hug. Kristi was not around when Molly and Weston first got together but I assumed no introduction was needed as I figured they probably still saw each other at school.

I had not noticed that Kyle was not here until Kristi asked the question. I knew they had no contact since they drifted their separate ways, but I was surprised at the way she worded her question.

"So where is that conceited bastard? Don't you all carpool down together?" She asked in a slightly heated voice. Weston looked around the room at each of us. He seemed a little worried about how the evening would go after hearing the tone of her voice.

Molly finally answered "He's coming later. His dad had some things he wanted him to do first. He said we'd have to eat without him."

Accepting the answer, we all sat down and ate dinner and after we finished the meal, we all took up different tasks to get the kitchen cleaned and plates into the dishwasher. Everyone was enjoying the drink of choice for the evening and it was decided to just hang here for the night rather than go out and have to deal with the tourists.

We played some games and chatted the night away. Weston and Molly had filled us in on their weeks activities while Kristi brought us up to date on her relationship with Keith the graduate from the Naval Academy. We were all laughing about my recounting the whole golf ball incident from back in February when Kyle finally made his entrance just after midnight. He was not alone.

"Vivian baby, wait until you see the view of the Bay from our little back porch, or deck, whatever you want to call it. You'll love it."

When we heard the name Vivian the five of us exchanged looks and then laughed understanding that the letter V might be crossed off the alphabet tonight, except for Kristi of course. She did not seem amused by the female visitor accompanying Kyle. She took on a sly smile and I could see the wheels turning in her head. She stood up from the dining table and went to meet Kyle before he reached us all. Seeing her stand, I tried my best to stop her, as if anyone could.

"Kristi! No!" I yelled to her trying to grab her as she dashed by.

She spun around me avoiding my grasp. "What? I am just going to say hi." Then darted to meet Kyle. Kyle rounded the corner and saw us all and was obviously shocked when he saw Kristi coming, and the look in her eyes.

"Hi Honey" She said sweetly then kissed him. Our mouths fell open, including Vivian's. "Did you miss me?" Kyle backed away from the embrace.

"Kristi what are you doing? And what are you doing here?" He was calm. That was a good at least.

"How nice to invite your cab driver in for a minute." She turned to Vivian, a rather well put together redhead, "Vivian thanks for driving him home in his drunken state." Then she gave her $10. "I hope that is a good enough tip. I am sure you must be going since you're working, and we shouldn't keep you." She turned Vivian towards the door ushering her along.

"Kristi stop!" Kyle yelled. I went and grabbed Kristi and started escorting her by the arm back to the table. She was not ready to leave Vivian or Kyle and did her best to avoid my pulling her away from the situation. I held fast though and was able to get her heading back to the rest of the group.

"Funny. I'll give you credit for that" I said to her in a hushed voice.

"Bye Vivian." She yelled back towards the hallway that she had left Kyle and Vivian standing in.

Kyle turned to Vivian "I am sorry about that. You should probably go." He knew with Kristi here he would have to attempt a V another time.

"Yeah, I think so. Call me this weekend if you can." She replied than walked out the door that Kyle had opened for her. Kyle watched as Vivian made her way down the street towards the closest bus stop then he closed the front door once he saw she had reached it. When Kyle walked into the dining area, we all tried our best to continue the game of Life we had been partially playing. Kyle, hands on his hips, did not look impressed with us. Kristi finally broke the silence and the tension.

"I'm sorry about Vivian. She seemed like a nice girl." Her sarcastic tone was evident, and it was obvious she was not sorry the least bit.

"Why should you care? What about Kevin?" He replied.

"Kevin?" She asked back wondering who Kevin was.

"Kevin! or Kenny, or Kendal, or whatever his name is." He clarified in a heated voice. Kyle was starting to get worked up. In all the time they had been together they never had arguments, not heated ones at least. His tone was one I had never heard him use before with Kristi.

"Keith?" She asked maintaining a calm demeanor.

"Whatever."

"What about him?"

"You don't see me interfering with your love interests." He said heatedly. "I must have really made an impression on her boys. She can't get passed K" he said pleased with this thought referencing his alphabet game as if Kristi were playing it too.

"V isn't that impressive either" Kristi said responding as if she understood what he was referring to. We all knew from her voice she was quite hurt understanding how many girls that would make going from K to V since her.

"Baby I started back at A." Kyle replied knowing that would hurt even more, and it did.

She calmly stood. Excused herself. Went into the kitchen and opened the refrigerator grabbing the eggs. I stood as we all watched her.

"No Kristi! No throwing food!" I yelled as she threw an egg at Kyle smacking him in the head. He turned and looked at her, then smiled. She dropped the eggs seeing the expression on his face and bolted past his arms attempting to grab her and ran up the stairs. Kyle chased after her. She ran into their old room and we heard the door slam shut. What we did not hear were any voices after the closing of the door. We all stood silently waiting to hear anything from upstairs. Nothing. For ten minutes nothing.

"Well, they're either strangling each other or making out. One of the two." Molly said breaking our silence.

"At least it was only one egg this time. When food gets involved with them when arguing it can take a week to find everything that was thrown." Weston added. Then it happened, the soft sounds of moaning from both.

"How does he do that?" Sydney asked to no one in particular.

"You're assuming it was him. Maybe she initiated it." I offered up.

Weston shook his head in disbelief. "Never a dull moment here." He smiled then added "I love it here."

Me too I thought. Me too.

40

The next morning, we were all nursing headaches. Weston and I were sitting on the couch while Molly and Sydney were propped on our laps. Heads together trying to ease the aches from the previous night.

"I'm thinking a vodka OJ might help" Syd said into my shoulder. She kissed me then went into the kitchen to fix herself something to hopefully help her hangover. She asked if we all wanted one and we all agreed by moaning. Everyone looked as good as they felt after a long night of drinking.

"Worst part is we didn't even get any last night." Weston moaned. Sydney shot me a look to see if I would agree with the sentiment. I remained silent knowing better than to disagree or say anything for that matter.

"Speak for yourselves boys." Kyle said all smiles while making his way down the stairs.

"Easy tiger." Kristi added slapping his shoulder following behind him. She too was smiling. They looked remarkably well. I stared at their smiling faces. It was a little irritating that they looked so good, so happy, and so not hungover.

"Well?" I asked. Kristi sat next to me leaning her head on my shoulder while smiling. She looked surprisingly unaffected by her drinking the night before.

"Well, we talked. And we're good now." She said nonchalantly.

"Like back together"? Molly asked what we all wanted to know. Kyle plopped down on the loveseat.

"No. No. No. Nothing like that, but we aren't mad at each other either." Kye answered.

"We are friends. I won't C block him anymore and he won't interfere with my relationships either." Kristi added smiling at Kyle.

"As if that was ever an issue from me" he muttered.

"Long story short, we can be friends again." She added staring at him.

"And if we have sex than all the better" He added "But no strings"

"Easy there. Not like that will definitely happen" she said now glaring at him.

"But if it does than great!" He added smiling.

"Sure. Then great." She relented.

Weston, with his eyes closed, smiled. "I love it here."

1995

41

The rest of 1994 went by too fast. Things seemed almost normal, and life felt a little bit like it was worth living. I was not totally back to feeling entirely filled with joy as there always seemed to feel like there was a void in my heart. I knew it was because of Sarah, I mean I still love her, and I know I always will, and even though Sydney was as close to perfection as it gets, she will never be able to fill that void. Sarah, no matter how small, will always have a piece of my heart.

Summer though had been beautiful, and the Fall had been peaceful with winter taking over. Kristi made visits quite a few times and seemed to get along with Kyle as if nothing bad had ever happened. There was thought of an eventual reigniting of the relationship by the rest of us, but by the end of the Summer Keith had proposed and she had accepted. To say we were shocked would be an understatement and in the early part of September we all attended her wedding, even Kyle.

The speediness of the wedding had nothing to do with her being knocked up or anything like that. No, it had to do with Keith's deployment to California and it was a do it now or wait a couple of years type of thing. She knew what she wanted. She knew that she loved him. She knew that he would lover her for as long as she wanted and then some. She had told me once that when you know what you want than make it a reality. So, they did. I knew they would be together forever, and I knew I would miss my best friend.

Kyle was content to live the single life. He did not bring girls back to the house though preferring to go to theirs instead. He would tell us about his adventures every now and then but kept them to himself mostly. I could not tell if he was searching for love or lust, but he seemed in a better place emotionally.

Weston and Molly were still going on as well, although I kind of got the feeling that boredom was setting in and I was not entirely sure that they would be together for too much longer. I do not know how to describe it, but they just seemed.........quiet. It was like as if they had run out of things to talk about and now had to rely on experiences they would share to keep things moving forward. They could not just be still and enjoy the silence together any longer.

Syd and I were as good as can be. She was everything I wanted in a girlfriend and more. We spent every minute we could together doing one thing or another. She too though felt a little distant. I had not made much progress in my life decisions and part of me wondered if she was getting tired of waiting for me to turn my life around. The other possibility was that she was tired of not pursuing things that would make her future better and more stable as well. I mean let us face it, she did drop everything to move here two years ago at this point. That is a long time to put your own interests on hold for someone else. Even if you do love that person.

I know I need to start thinking about adulting, it was just so hard to do when I was still so melancholy at times. Still though, I knew it had to happen soon and so I returned to the local community college here for some classes majoring in education. I think I had decided on teaching as my future and Sydney seemed happier in seeing me take a step towards making life happen.

One full spring semester in and I noticed that I really was liking the school thing. No volleyball courts, no student activity center, just one main building where all the classes were held. That made things easier having less distractions. That summer I even enrolled for two classes deciding to not hamper the momentum I had built from the spring semester. The summer was full. Work, school, still doing the beach volleyball thing, and then of course trying to fit time in with Sydney as well.

It was tough on us at times. The time apart seemed to divide us a bit, not bring us together, and then when we were together it seemed stressful like trying to make up for time not spent together. It was not natural but felt forced and I could tell Syd was a little bit worried. For so long I had depended on her to keep me balanced and now I seemed to be doing well on my own. Maybe she missed that feeling of being needed? I do not know, but it does feel like there was a distance growing between us.

An interesting thing happened in June. Something that I was not proud of and felt a little out of control of the situation. It had been raining hard and both Weston and Sydney were at work. Molly was down for the week and was at the house by herself. When I came home from work, I wanted to go surfing as I knew the waves were good as I had walked across Coastal Highway and checked the surf out on my lunch break. Molly had asked if she could join me, and I agreed thinking nothing about it. I had lent her one of my boards and after about an hour we made our way out of the water to head home when the skies just opened up. I had never seen such a hard rain before while living at the beach. It reminded me of something that you would experience in the rain forests. It was a miserable experience trying to get out of the wetsuits and we tried our best to tie down the boards as best as we could.

The clothes that we had changed into were immediately drenched to the point of where we could have just stayed in the wetsuits and we had a good laugh about it when we got home. Molly went upstairs to change and since we were cold from the drenching, I decided to start a fire as soon as I got down from changing into some comfortable shorts. It was a fun day, and I will admit that I had never spent time together with Molly without Weston around at the same time, but it felt natural.

She had come down and seeing me on my knees trying to stoke the fire a bit she playfully came from the side of me and knocked me over then laughed as she saw me lose my balance and fall over onto my side. Not taking that too well, and still in a playful mood myself, I reached over and grabbed her with both hands around her ankles and pulled her hard. She lost her balance and fell forward landing on top of me. She looked down at me and got a serious look in her eyes.

"Would you mind if I did something? Something I've always wanted to do?" She asked me in a low soft voice that was just above a whisper.

"Sure!" I said still enjoying the day and not noticing the change in the mood around me. And then it happened. She kissed me. I was not expecting that to be what she had said she had always wanted to do, and it caught me off guard. It was a slow kiss, gentle, and on the softer side. It was not that it was bad, but since I was unaware that it was going to happen, I was not the most active participant either, and when she parted from me, she had a less than satisfied look on her face.

"Hmm. Not at all what I expected." She said in that soft voice still but sounding disappointed. I am not sure if my male pride kicked in or what, but I was a little offended and surprised even myself at what I said next.

"I'm sorry. You just caught me off guard. Let's try that again." I reached up and put my hand on the back of her head and pulled her back to me. This time I knew I had not failed in the attempt. This kiss was full of everything I could muster. Every feeling of love and romance I could generate and although I knew it was not really meant for her but to save the reputation of me that had entered her mind that I was probably a good kisser. I made sure to uphold that reputation and when we parted this time, I could see that her preconceived notions about kissing me had been surpassed well beyond what she was thinking what it might be like.

"Whoa" She said in a dreamy eyed state. "That was so much more than what I thought it would be. Thank you." She sat up straight on the floor allowing me to lean to the side on my elbow. "I've never had a kiss like that. Weston kisses like his final goal is sex, not with emotion or passion." She continued.

"You're welcome" I managed looking up at her somewhat pleased with her reaction to the second kiss.

"I've always loved you, David. I've always wished that we were together. I know that's impossible, but I needed to know at least what it would be like and now I know, and it makes me sad." She looked down at her hands in her lap. She had a very innocent look to her now. A look of helplessness really. A victim of her heart knowing that what her heart desires would never be a possibility and I could see the pain she was in.

I understood that look completely. It touched me in my soul seeing her so down hearted about the whole thing. I sat up, lifted her chin, and then kissed her again. This time softer, gentler, more like a return of the kiss that she had attempted the first time and she willingly returned it and as if the timing could not have been any worse, we were interrupted by the front door opening.

We parted as quickly as we could but there is no way that whoever just came through the door would not have seen the embrace. She quickly stood and made her way up the stairs passing Kyle by the door as she did so. She did not say anything, but I could see her brushing a tear off her cheek as she went up the stairs.

Kyle stood there smiling that crappy grin of his and when

he had heard the door to Weston's room close, he continued into the living room to apparently discuss the situation he walked in on. I did not say anything as he made his way to the couch never taking his eyes from me.

"So. What the hell was that?" He asked in a shocked voice.

I shook my head not entirely knowing myself. "I have no idea."

"You have no idea? It looked kind of mutual to me. There must have been something leading up to that?" He said in response as if not believing me. I filled him in on everything from going surfing, to her not being satisfied in her first attempt, my ego causing the second one, the feelings she expressed, and up to what he walked in on.

"Ok, I get everything except the last one. Why kiss her the last time? Was it a pity kiss?"

"No." I said disgusted by that thought.

"It was an... I don't know why. Not pity, but empathy. I know how she feels." I tried to explain.

"Wait, you love her too?" He asked not understanding.

"No. I understand loving someone that you know you'll never be with. Must be even harder on her since she is here with us all the time she can be. I'm right here in front of her and she is unable to do anything about it. At least for me Sarah is at a minimum two hours away if she's home and say six if she's at Frostburg." I sat there thinking about that for a moment. "I can't even imagine how hard it must be for her."

"What about Weston?" He asked. "Why is she staying with him if she is so in love with you?"

I shook my head again. "I don't know. Maybe she does love him. Or thinks she does." I thought about this for a moment then added "Or she's hoping that it will fill her enough to eventually forget about the one she does love." Kyle said nothing and then a thought occurred to me. "You aren't going to say anything to Weston, are you?" I asked a little bit too excitedly. He just stared at me for a moment.

"No. I won't tell Weston. Or Sydney" He emphasized the or as if correcting me for asking his silence for the wrong person. I looked up at him surprised by his correction of my thoughts. Why had I not included Sydney?

"Just don't make this a habit." Kyle said to me as we both turned towards the sound of the front door opening.

"Make what a habit?" We heard Weston say as he walked into to living room. Thinking fast I made up the best answer I could.

"Molly and I went surfing and I lent her Skippy's board. I dinged it when I almost ran her over once."

"Molly surfed?" He asked surprised.

"Well, she tried. I think she had fun though." I answered back building on the lie. He smiled at the thought of his girl-friend being on a surfboard. It was his turn to cook dinner tonight and once he had taken of his sandals, he went about gathering the ingredients that he would use calling upstairs just once asking Molly to join him. She did not. It was not that much longer when Sydney got home and when she came through the front door, I greeted her with a kiss. A small peck really.

"Wow. That was heartfelt" She said smiling half joking and half serious.

Weston was cooking spaghetti tonight. We ate that a lot. It was a cheap meal that is easy to prepare that we all seemed to like. And while taking turns making dinners, we all had our own ways of making things. Weston opted for a more traditional ap-proach with a tomato sauce and meatballs and although it was delicious, I had hardly eaten any of it. I looked over and noticed that Molly had twirled a bunch and shifted food around her plate but had barely eaten anything as well and although there was conversation happening all through dinner, I could tell that she had not heard a word of it.

"Everything alright Molly?" Weston asked. Molly looked up from her private thoughts as if unaware as to why he would ask that question. "You've barely eaten anything? Too spicy?" Weston asked trying to start up a conversation that she would want to be involved in.

"No. No. Everything is fine." She said trying to smile. "I'm tired really. I think I'm just going to go to bed." She said excusing herself from the table. We all watched as she made her way up the stairs and when the door to Weston's room closed, he too excused himself and went up as well.

"What is going on here?" Sydney asked in a questioning tone as if everyone but her knew something but did not want to say.

"I'm not sure." Kyle said. "But I'm betting whatever it is will be better by the morning." Kyle shot me a look and whether it was the guilt I had over the kiss or the understanding of the sadness in Molly's heart over a love she knew she could never have I felt awful as well.

"I'm feeling a little bit like a cold is coming on, I think I'm going to turn in as well." I said to the two of them.

"Everything ok Babe?" Sydney asked concerned over my apparent mood or possible illness. "It's barely 8 o'clock."

"Yeah. Yeah." I said reassuring her as best as I could. "I'm just feeling a little off. Probably from being out in the rain today."

I stood up from the table and kissed Sydney on the top of the head and walked up to my room. On the way up the stairs I could hear Kyle and Sydney joking about being the only two left to clean up after dinner and as I closed the door to my room, I could hear music downstairs playing and the sounds of the kitchen being cleaned up.

As I laid down on my bed, I could not help but think about how Molly might be feeling, and my heart ached a little for her. And though I knew I could not return her love for me; I could be the friend that she needed. I would do as much as she wanted and as much as I could without crossing any lines and one day, I knew I must tell Weston of this day and what happened, but that day could wait. If Molly was with him there was no point in taking that away from her. I would not take away her source of comfort, or at least I hoped he was a comfort. I wanted nothing but the best for her and hopefully she would be able to find someone that could take my place in her heart.

42

It was a great summer for the most part. Sun, surf, and sand a plenty and many good times were had with my little group of roommates. August was always a sad month for me as I knew it signaled the end of summer was nearing. I did love the fall months at the beach, but it was always hard knowing the warmer days were behind us.

Life was happening or I should say adulting was happening. I was going to continue classes this fall, and Sydney was also going to go back to school. Part time at least back at UMBC. It was a start, and her parents were happy about her decision feeling she had wasted enough time at the beach. We had talked about it and we had both decided that she was going to stay here part time during the fall. Tuesday through Thursday back home in Severna Park and Thursday evening through Monday night here with me. Three nights alone, well sort of.

Weston had decided to stay here for the fall. The way his classes worked if he went full time next spring he could graduate in the spring. He felt it made no sense to drive back and forth for a part time schedule for two semesters. Save the gas and move back in January made more sense to him. As Weston decided to stay, so too did Molly. Upon hearing her decision to stay I did not know what to think about it. Was she into self-torture as much as I was?

Three nights alone without Syd I guess I should have said. I knew I would miss her. We had grown comfortable together, but not passionate, and though I felt there was a distance growing between us, I still would miss her. Heck maybe this would be good for us. Absence makes the heart grow fonder kind of thing?

Wednesday August 16th came, and I was busy at work with inventory. I had come in at 2pm and knew I would be there kind of late. We could not get much counting done because of how busy it is at the store during these summer months and so the bulk of it was done before opening or after closing. I had always like inventory time at every retail job I had because it was fun to me. Kind of like a party at least to me.

I was busy with a customer when I noticed a pair of motherly types walk into the store, one of which I knew quite well. When she saw me, a huge smile came across her face and she made her way over to me. I returned the smile, genuinely glad to see her.

"Hi Mrs. Fulton. How have you been?" I asked Sarah's mom. She looked me up and down as if looking to see if I had changed much since Christmas of 1992. Sarah and I had lived together until April of 1993, but I had not seen her parents since the Christmas before. Wow, had it been that long I thought? Over two years since my last contact with Sarah? It did not seem that long, and yet it seemed an eternity as well.

"David! How have you been? Still living here, I guess." She continued to look at me, but I could not tell what she was thinking exactly. She seemed so happy to see me for some unknown reason.

"Yeah, still here" I replied then added "But back in school." Hoping for what? Approval maybe? For some reason I felt the need to make her proud. She had always been so sweet to me before and I did not like it when she was upset or unhappy with me. Quite different than with Syd's parents. I could care less what they think of me, but Mrs. Fulton was different. I wanted her approval. Ached for it really.

"Oh, that's great David! I am glad to see you planning for life after Volleyball." She said granting my wish of her approval. I wanted to ask about Sarah, but I could not find the words and as if reading my mind, she took the conversation in that direction. "Sarah graduated from Frostburg last May, she got a job as a teacher in Prince George's County. She starts in a couple of weeks, well she has already started, but the new school year starts in a couple of weeks." She seemed a little nervous for some reason. I knew I was. I did not know how Sarah explained our last break from each other to her parents. Was it mutual or was I the bad guy? I mean it was not mutual, and I had been the bad guy, but had she relayed that information to them?

"Oh, that's amazing! I'm so happy for her" I replied. As much as I had wanted to hear about Sarah it somehow felt awkward. It fell silent for a moment as if neither of us knew what to say but neither of us wanted the conversation to end either. Then she brightened as if a thought just occurred to her.

"You know she's coming into to town in a few hours?"

I thought about this for a moment before replying "Really? Gosh I haven't seen her in a couple of years."

She shook her head as if confirming her private thought. "I'm going to bring her to the store" She looked up at me as the thought occurred to her that I may not want to see her "That is if you're ok with that?"

I did not hesitate "That would be great! I'd love to see her!" I answered way to excitedly.

She smiled back at me then patted my back. "I'll see you in a bit. Don't you worry about a thing." Worry about a thing? I thought to myself why would I worry? Maybe because of how things had ended?

She gathered up her companion who had been wondering around looking at some of the clothes we offered before offering up her goodbyes. I stood and watched her exit out of the store and make her way down the mall hallway wondering to myself if she would truly come back or not, and with Sarah. Would Sarah want to see me? Would her mom even tell her why they were coming here?

After a few moments of these private thoughts my manager Ruth called for me asking who I had been talking to. I told her who it was, and she smiled at me. Ruth was old enough to be my mom, and sometimes acted like our moms to me and my fellow coworkers, but she meant well. She knew who Sarah was and what she meant to me.

"If she comes" she said grinning at me "you take as much time as you need. Don't worry about us, we will be counting all week, so a little time now won't break us."

The next few hours I found myself checking the entrance way too much. So much so I was losing track of counts and Ruth was starting to get frustrated with me. Finally, just before 7pm, I saw Sarah run past the store window and into the front entrance. She smiled at me widely and waved. I saw Mrs. Fulton trailing behind trying to keep up but failing to do so. Sarah did not say a word to me, and she did not wait for me to speak either, she just ran to me and embraced me in a hug. It was a tight embrace and did not end when her mom finally made it up behind her.

"I think I'll just leave you two alone" Mrs. Fulton said seeing that the embrace might not end anytime soon. Sarah finally parted from me and we stood staring into each other's eyes "You'll make sure she gets back to the condo?" Her mom asked me. Sarah raised her eyebrows as if also asking and I could tell my heart was in trouble yet again. I held her gaze while answering yes in a solemn voice as if giving some kind of sacred oath or vow. Her mom nodded once as if satisfied with my response, then turned around and made her way out of the store. Mrs. Fulton seemed pleased with herself and I could see her grinning from ear to ear as she headed left in the mall and I assumed back to her car.

I turned back to Sarah and I could tell her eyes had never wavered from mine. I took in the full site of her. She was wearing a red Polo shirt that had a dark blue horse and matched her dark blue Guess jeans perfectly. Her outfit was completed with a pair of simple white sandals that looked like she had worn them often over the last couple of years. Not exactly dingy, but comfortable looking, and she looked like she belonged here at the beach. Her hair was still long, and she wore it parted from left to right. It was curlier than I remembered but looked amazing on her. Her blue eyes were still the bluest I had ever seen, and it is not that I had forgotten how beautiful they were, but I found myself awe struck by them as if it were my first time seeing them all over again.

"What time do you get off work?" She asked still staring at me. I broke her gaze to look over at Ruth. She and another co-worker named Bonnie were watching me interested in the story that was playing out in front of them.

"Go on David. Get out of here." She yelled over to me smiling widely. Everyone was smiling it seemed, except for Sarah and I, we were much too intense at the moment to be smiling.

"Want to get out of here?" She asked still looking into my eyes. It occurred to me that I had yet to speak to her. The only word she had heard me say was a simple yes to her mother. I mustered up the strongest voice I could then barely muttered a one-word answer. "Yes" I replied still on the meeker side of the spectrum. She came up beside me and took my hand in hers and lead me out the store door and into the mall.

I will never understand this connection she and I have, nor will I ever be able to describe it correct enough to do it justice, but it was true back in 1988 and apparently still true in 1995 that my heart will always be Sarah Fulton's. I can try to replace her, I can try and hide it, I can try to bury her away into the forgotten depths of my mind, but the undeniable reality is that she and I are connected in a way only told of in story's. Although I had tried to move on from her and rebuild my life, I once again knew life would never be complete without her in it and as we walked hand in hand down through the mall I felt whole again,

and I was happy.

43

When we reached her car, she turned to me and broke the silence. We had been walking slowly through the mall and out to the parking lot as if going at a normal pace might break the spell we both were currently under. No words had been spoken either, again for the fear of disrupting this moment. This had been one of those "enjoy the silence" moments that we used to have and in that silence a reconnecting of our souls was occurring that I knew both of us wanted and yet feared at the same time. Fear of knowing our hearts again were exposed and knowing that we stood the chance of being hurt yet again. Oh, how I loved these moments with her, these new beginnings we would have, and yet how I hated them as well. Had I made enough progress in my life, grown enough in myself, in order to make this work? To be what she so rightly deserves? I have always been good at loving her when we were together, but it is when we had to be apart that I struggled. And life? I am still such a child in that regard. Adulting is only now starting to really happen for me. Could she wait? Should she? All things I guess we will find out together soon enough. Right now though, I just simply want to enjoy her for however long that may be.

"What would you like to do?" She asked still with such a serious look in her eyes and on her face.

"I don't care. Just take me with you." I answered. This made her smile finally. A slight smile, but a smile none the less.

"Are you hungry?" She asked me. I answered that I was not. "Neither am I." She looked down at the ground as if fumbling with what to say next.

"How about we get your car back to where you are staying, grab a blanket out of my car, and just enjoy the sunset? Be still with each other by the water." I suggested. Truth be told I did not want the crowds of the boardwalk, or restaurants, or anywhere else people congregate here in town. I wanted to be alone with her. I wanted, if this possibly was a closing of one of life's chapters in our books, to be able to focus 100% on her. I wanted to be able to memorize every line of her face, the sound of her voice, the curves of her body, and the blueness of her eyes. I knew my heart would never forget her. I wanted to make sure my mind would have her image burned into it as well.

I had started that process the moment she turned to face me by her car and when she looked back up at me, she could still see the seriousness of my gaze.

"Ok. I think that sounds perfect. I don't want to leave you yet though." She reached out and grabbed my other hand holding both of mine in hers.

"I'll ride with you then. We can grab the blanket out of my car, return yours, and I can bus it back to mine later." I suggested thinking this to be an excellent solution to the problem. She smiled again and nodded her affirmation.

We parted so that we could get into the car and make our plan happen and less than ten minutes later we were parking her car at the condo where she was staying. I remembered the place well once we got there and could not help but smile when I saw the pool. I stopped by the gate that was next to it as the memory of her kissing me and then me dunking her flooded back from wherever memories are stored. The smile turned into a small chuckle at the thought and Sarah looked around wondering what would have made me laugh. When she saw the pool, a smile formed on her face as well.

"Come on David" she said pulling me along by the hand. "We can check the pool out some other time. I might even let you dunk me."

We did not bother stopping at the condo. We parked, grabbed the blanket, and went towards the water. When we got there, we chose a place to sit looking out towards the ocean. The waves were long and rolling and were on the louder side tonight. The kind of waves tourist come for and expect to see as no one likes it when the ocean looks like a lake. The time was passing 8:30pm and darkness was starting to creep in. Maybe only another 30 minutes or so of light to really enjoy the view. After that we would have to rely on the white caps breaking on the shore and the sounds they would make to enjoy.

As we sat on the blanket facing the water, I could feel her leaning towards me slowly as if asking permission to be closer. I grabbed her hand and draped the bond made into her lap. She moved closer and laid her head on my shoulder. As we watched the sky turn from vibrant colors from the sunset to the blackness the night offers both of us were content to just be still. Once dark a small breeze had set in which was just enough to make it a little on the cool side. I noticed her small goose bumps and offered the other blanket we had brought as a "just in case" type thing. We both knew how the temperature could change from perfect to slightly cool in an instant.

"I have a better idea." She said switching her position from sitting to laying on her left side still facing the water. "Come lay next to me and then we can both use the blanket" she added. Looking down at her I could not help but do as she asked and so I laid next to her.

I was propped up on my left elbow so I could continue to study her face, even if it were the side of her face since she was looking out to the water. I pressed my body up against her and wrapped my right arm over her which she then quickly took my hand and pulled it up near her face. Feeling my body close she pressed hers to me getting as close as we could to each other while still wearing clothes.

"What are you doing up there?" She asked turning her

head slightly as if a little unhappy that my other arm and head were not as close to her as they could be.

"I'm looking at you Sarah. I don't ever want to forget the way you look right now." She did not look satisfied with that answer.

"Come closer. This is not goodbye David. I'm here until Sunday morning. You can do that later, but for now be close to me." I did as she asked kissing the side of her head by her ear as I made my way down from my position. I slid my left arm underneath her and pressed the side of my face to the back of her head. "Thank you" she whispered in appreciation for doing what she had asked.

After about an hour I could feel her shift a bit pulling my arms even tighter to her as if attempting to get closer still. "This feels so right. So good. I've forgotten how perfect things can be." She whispered. So had I, I thought to myself, this moment was perfect and as if neither one of us wanted to cheapen it in any way we both remained silent.

Lost in the embrace and in private unspoken thoughts the time drifted by. I could not help but wonder what she was thinking about. Was it me? Or the being back at the beach that she had loved so much when she lived here briefly? I was praying it was me, but I could never read her the way she could me. She always knew exactly what I was thinking and feeling. I am sure she already knew how hopelessly I was in love with her yet again and when it passed 2am we both knew what needed to happen. Sharing one tender kiss we both stood from the blankets, brushed off the sand, and walked hand in hand back to the condo.

Without saying a word, the whole walk back, I walked her up the 2 flights of stairs to the door, gave her another soft kiss, and then watched her enter the condo. We did not break our hands until the door closing had forced the issue. I walked back down the stairs and stood near the pool where I had a view of the room that I knew she would be occupying and noticed the light was on. I stayed there until the light went off some fifteen minutes later and then walked slowly up the street and made my way to the closest bus stop. Along the way I could not contain the smile on my face. Thinking back on the night and how intimate it was.

All I have ever wanted was one more of those perfect moments with Sarah and tonight had been just that. I had no idea what it meant or where this was going but I was excited for the rest of the week and when I finally made it home, I walked in and went straight to the back deck. I grabbed a blanket, sat in the lounge chair, and staring off into the night sky and the bay I drifted off to sleep thinking only of Sarah.

44

Morning came and with it the inevitable reality of where I live and with whom I am living with. I was expecting to be bombarded with an assault of questions on my unexpected disappearance last night and I was quite surprised when I came in through the back door and saw only Kyle standing there.

"What time is it?" I asked in a groggy voice.

"Almost 10am" He answered while drinking his glass of OJ. He was watching me intently as if waiting for me to offer up information about what happened last night and when I walked past him to grab some milk from the fridge he apparently knew right away.

"Jesus, you smell like Sarah." He eyed me as if wondering how that could be possible and for confirmation.

"Yeah. Long story. Is Syd awake yet?" I asked knowing I needed to deal with this. He had a serious look on his face.

"No. She went home after work yesterday and won't be back until Saturday. Remember? Helping with the volleyball camp at UMBC?" He asked as if I should have known. I did but had forgotten. "She called earlier, but you were still sleeping" He added. That was good at least as I would not have to deal with this for a bit.

I was lost in private thought when he asked me if I was going to tell him about yesterday. I sat on the couch and told him the whole story. Her mom coming into work, Sarah coming later, the walk to the car, the beach, the silence, the kiss goodnight, and the not wanting our hands to part even after the door forced us to.

"Damn." He said quietly. It was not a good damn. It was not a congratulations type thing like "Damn that's amazing", No, this was a "Damn, all the work to get you over her and it's all been for nothing. You, We, Everyone, are all right back at square one and someone is going to get hurt." I understood.

"You going to see her again?" He asked me.

"I'd like to, but I didn't think about getting her number at the condo so I don't know how that will work unless I just show up." Seems to be a habit of mine, the forgetting to get her number so I can attempt to see her again. Somehow, she had always managed to get mine though and contact me and is if on cue the phone rang. I jumped up off the couch and ran to grab it.

"Hello?" I asked into the phone.

"Oh, good it's you. I won't have to ask for Weston after all" Sarah replied. That made me smile.

"What are your plans?" I asked into the phone.

"None. You?"

"I'm yours if you want." I answered back. I had decided I would take the rest of the week off to be with Sarah. Damn the inventory.

"Great! Are you ready?" She asked me.

"I'll jump in the shower and head over." After she told me to just come up and knock, we hung up and I went to go get ready. I could hear Kyle swearing to himself in the kitchen.

As quickly as I could I set to the task of getting ready and making good on my time estimate. I was there within 30 minutes. I parked in an open space next to her building and in my excitement of seeing her I took the stairs two at a time. When I got to her door I knocked eagerly. I could hear a muffled voice telling me to come on in, so I did. As soon as I opened the door, I could hear a hair dryer being used. Sarah peeked out from the bathroom near her room and told me to come on in. I made my way to her where she was getting ready in the open bathroom and turned around quickly when I noticed she was wearing nothing but a nighty while getting ready. She laughed at my reaction.

"Oh stop. Not like you haven't seen me before." She said still drying her hair but turned to look at me and allow me to look at her.

I could not help myself. I turned to face her. My eyes went huge at the sight of her and how that little blue silk nighty looked against her body. She smiled as if knowing exactly what I was thinking. It was her Superpower with me, she always knew everything. I could never keep thoughts or emotions to myself as she would always know them. Sometimes even before I knew them. She set the hair dryer down and rushed into my arms and kissed me. It was one of those kisses that said exactly what was wanted and expected and right there on the floor in front of the bathroom door, we made love.

Once we parted from the embrace that always follows making love, she informed me that her parents were out for the day but that they had invited us to dinner. I told her that sounded great, and I would make sure we got back in time. Since it was almost 2pm it only gave us a couple of hours before needing to get back so we could help if needed. Our options, being so slim due to lack of time, we decided to just walk up the beach for a bit and catch up about the last two years.

It was a beautiful day with sunny skies and only 85 degrees. The ocean though was still compared to the evening before, like a lake, with tiny little waves only breaking at your feet if you chose to walk by the water. Walking and talking while holding hands we would stop every now and then so she could grab a seashell or two.

"Not that I'm complaining David, but I am surprised that you wanted to do this."

"This?" I asked not knowing what she meant.

"I tell you we have the condo for a couple of hours to ourselves and you choose to go for a walk with me instead?" She said slyly indicating that maybe we could have stayed in instead. I thought about that for a moment.

"I'm simply happy to be here with you. I don't care what we do as long as it's together" I replied with conviction in my voice. That was honestly the truth. Although I loved the intimate moment we just shared, I have never required that of her. If it happened it happened kind of thing, but that in no way means I did not want her or not desire her. I absolutely did with every fiber of my being, but I would never pressure her about it. Besides, it was never an issue with us. Our intimate lives was healthier than most. She looked over at me as if making sure I was telling the truth.

"Hmmm. Good answer, but maybe I would have wanted to stay there?" She replied smiling.

"Then you should have said so." I said without looking over at her. She dropped my hand and shoved me into the water a bit then used both hands to splash water up at me.

"Now you're going to get it!" I yelled at her and charged her picking her up in my arms and carried her off towards the water that was now knee deep to me.

"No David. Please No." She begged a little. I was carrying her high and in front of me. Her backside resting in my forearms and her stomach pressed to my face. She was wearing a pair of white shorts and her black Bodyglove bikini top with a tank top draped over her shoulder. Her hair was pulled back in a ponytail in order to catch as much of the sun as she could and just the few short hours we had been walking, her skin was starting to look sun kissed.

Her eyes were pleading into mine as well as if her voice were not convincing enough. I allowed her to slip down through my arms but did not release her from my arms and when her feet finally reached the ground she too was now knee deep in the water. Looking into each other's eyes another moment of seriousness came over us both as once again we found ourselves face to face.

Sarah closed her eyes and moved her lips to mine. And as the kiss continued, the water rushing past us, holding each other close, I knew that she still loved me. When two people are as connected as we are you feel it in certain ways, like in the touch of a hand, a look in the eyes, the feel of a kiss, and this time I knew exactly how she felt. When we parted from the kiss, she had a dreamy look in her eyes.

"David I"

"I know Sarah, I know. You don't need to say anything." She parted from the embrace entirely walking back out of the water and towards the condo. She looked back at me.

"What are we going to do? How is this going to work?" She asked in an exasperated tone as if reality was setting in. I ran up to her and forced a hug on her.

"Hey. Hey. Hey. Stop this. We will figure things out. It doesn't have to be right now though. Let's just enjoy each other. Here. Now. We can talk about those things later. Be still with me." I pleaded with her trying to get her to relax.

She submitted and allowed herself to return the hug. After a long minute or so I could feel her body ease and the tension from it was released. Only then did I allow the hug to end. We took hold of each other's hands and made our way back to the condo. Neither one of us talked but we would share looks at each other and smile occasionally squeezing each other's hand and by the time we walked in through the front door just before 6pm I could tell she was back to her normal cheerful self.

45

Dinner was nice and simple. Hamburgers and Hot Dogs on the grill with different potato chip flavors to choose from. Mr. and Mrs. Fulton had asked what we had spent our time doing that afternoon and I could see her mom smile as Sarah and I exchanged glances not sure of what all to say. We stuck with walking and sitting on the beach as a good enough answer.

"Dad you should have seen it though." She said excitedly "David was going to toss me into the water again." Her father eyed me from the side as he was in mid bite when she told on me. I jokingly kicked her under the table which made her smile. Her mom not missing anything seemed pleased with the playful banter.

"What is it with you and your fascination with dunking my daughter?" Mr. Fulton asked after he had swallowed his bite. Pleased with herself Sarah stuck her tongue out at me.

"She's kind of a brat Mr. Fulton" I replied after seeing her little display of her tongue. She kicked me now only much harder than I had her.

He chuckled "Don't I know it." Shaking his head, he took another bite. Again, her mother smiled. Sarah did not.

"Are you two hanging out tonight?" Her mom asked.

"No" replied Sarah pretending to be hurt by my comment and after about 10 seconds she could not contain her feigned attitude and began to grin widely.

"Actually, we hadn't talked about it yet" She said answering her mother's question. "He hasn't asked me yet." I looked over at her as she bit into some chips crunching loudly as if to emphasize her point of how inconsiderate I must be for taking so long to ask her out on another date.

"If she can find it in her heart to forgive me, I would love to take her out for the night." Sarah smiled at that and looked up at me. "I was too busy enjoying my time with her today to think about this evening, that and I was unsure if you all already had plans, I didn't want to interfere with them if you had. Long story short, I'll keep her out of your hair for the night if she would like to go out with me." Again, her mom smiled to herself.

"Please do. We could use a brat free night, isn't that right dear?" Mr. Fulton asked looking over at her mother.

"Dad!" She exclaimed acting as if she was shocked by his comment.

"Oh yes. She is free if she likes. We will stay here and play some Scrabble." Her mom replied freeing Sarah for the evening. The loving gaze we had been sharing as of late returned. The one that excluded everything else but each other, and when both her parents saw how we were looking at each other her mom told us to leave, that they could clean up after dinner. We quickly emptied our plates, she changed into a 3/4 length sleeved summer shirt that hung off her shoulders, grabbed a sweatshirt as a just in case, and we were out the door. With no plan as to what we were going to do we both were as giddy as we were back in High-school as we made our way to my car.

46

"Drive" Sarah commanded once we got into my car. I turned on the car and decided to head south and out of town. Once we got on the road, she reached over and took my hand in hers. I enjoyed this as it was always our way. To be always touching in some little way when together. Even if it was just a foot or a finger, if we were touching it made it feel like everything was ok, that life was somehow easier. Once she saw me head out of town on Rte. 50, she looked over at me.

"Where are we going?" She asked.

"Shantytown" I answered. She used to love walking the docks there and looking in the little shops. Being almost 8pm I was not sure if any would still be open or not, but we could still walk the dock.

I parked my car and we got out walking the little grouping of stores. Some were still open, and we would walk into them when we could. Sarah was content though to walk the dock and peer into the windows. When it got dark, we made our way back to the car and headed back into town and to the boardwalk. She has always loved the more touristy attractions of Ocean City whereas I tended to steer clear of them.

I parked at the inlet so that we could walk as much of the busier parts as she would like and when we came to the rides down by the street, we both laughed as we watched the Zipper ride flip and circle its riders.

"No Sarah. No Zipper" I said pulling her by the hand past the ride.

"Oh, I have no desire to revisit that experience" She said

gripping my hand even tighter. We gave each other a look though when we got to the Fun House. I knew this did interest her. I bought us the tickets and we took our places next to each other choosing to go at the same time and make it a race. She is always such the competitor with me. This still has not changed about her.

When the attendant told us to go, she shot up the foot obstacle that lifts you higher faster than I had ever seen her do it before. She must have been practicing I thought. I was not as good at it as I used to be, and she easily took a huge lead. Once I managed to make it up the first obstacle, I only ever saw the back side of her as she managed all the obstacles with ease. It seemed like she was waiting for me, not starting the next one until she saw me enter the one she had just finished. And when I finally got through the last little obstacle, I saw her standing before the giant blow up slide that ends the Fun House experience as you take the slide back to the ground floor. She was standing there with a huge grin across her face. She was definitely pleased with herself and at how badly she had beaten me. I made my way to her not hearing her gloating.

"HaHaHa I totally kicked your..." She was saying as I pushed her backwards and down the slide. Then I jumped down the slide as well.

"Oh my God David. You did not just push me down that slide." Now I was the one laughing. Her hair was standing up in places from the static electricity from going down the blow-up slide.

"I'm sorry Sarah." I said still laughing "I guess I should have let you have your moment."

She stood up as quickly as she could brushing herself off as she went. She did not look happy. I stood as well and hurriedly made my way towards her reaching for her hand as I got beside her. She reluctantly gave it. She was silent as we continued to walk down the boardwalk and I could see she had a slight frown on her face.

"I'm sorry Sarah. I just wasn't prepared to get beaten by you so badly. I mean you kicked my ass. By a lot. Like showed no mercy to me at all and I was not ready for that." Her frown quickly changed back to a smile at my retelling of the events that had just unfolded.

"You're a sore loser David. Like really bad." She did not look over at me yet.

"I know, and I'm sorry. Let me make it up to you?" I pleaded with her. She looked over at me finally before speaking.

"I guess Ice Cream might be a good start. Dumser's always seems to make things a little better." Luckily, we were approaching one on the boardwalk. I forgot she knew the boardwalk as well as I did and part of me thought she suggested it because it was right there in front of us. We ordered our shakes and continued to walk. Occasionally we would stop in a store, or play a game of chance, sometimes go into one of the arcades and play some skeeball but mostly we walked. Hand in hand, side by side, as close as ever.

The shops do not stay open all night though and by midnight we made our way off the boardwalk and onto the beach. I was surprised to see that down by the water it was quite peaceful and seemed void of people. Sarah and I were alone.

"I let you win you know?" Her head turned slowly to me. I smiled since we both knew the truth and when she saw my expression and knew the truth of the matter, she pushed me down, climbed on top of me, and there for the second time that day, we made love.

47

It was after 4am by the time we got back to the condo. I was sure we would hear about this, but everyone was asleep when we got there. She looked at me as I stayed inside by the door as she checked the rest of the place to make sure we were as alone as we could get. When she came back to me, she took my hand and pulled me into her room, closing the door quietly behind her.

"Passion has never been our problem" She said looking at me as I still stood there not exactly sure of what we were doing. Then she hugged me and remained there in my arms.

"That's the truth for sure." I replied enjoying the embrace.

"Are we spending the day together tomorrow?" She asked into my shoulder.

"Yes, we need to celebrate your birthday." She looked up at me.

"My birthday was last Sunday."

"I know, but I didn't get the chance to celebrate it with you, so we are doing it tomorrow."

"You've done that trick before and although I absolutely loved it back then can we just leave that perfect memory in the past and not ruin it by trying to do a repeat of it? Can we just have a fun Friday together?" I understood what she meant. Why mess with a perfect thing?

"Sure Babe, whatever you want." She sighed and put her head back on my shoulder.

"Uhg, you know what that does to me when you call me

'Babe', I melt every time I hear you call me that."

"I know. That's why I said that." I replied smugly.

"And I'm the brat?" She asked quietly.

We decided for me to sleep on the couch for the night and that I was not allowed to wake her up in the morning. If her parents woke me up in the morning than too bad. I thought that was rather cruel myself. It was not entirely my fault that we got back so late, but I certainly was not going to complain about why we got back so late either. We kissed once and she pushed me out her door as we said goodnight.

I slept until 11am and was surprised to see Sarah was out on the balcony having a cup of coffee already. I got up and made my way over to her sliding the glass door to the balcony open. Her head turned to me when she heard the door sliding. She was in simple sweats and a T-shirt, I assumed the outfit she chose to sleep in. I leaned over and kissed her good morning.

"Where are your parents?" I asked her. She handed me a note saying that they were heading out for the day and they would be having crabs for dinner if we both were interested and to be back by 4 if we were.

"What do you think?" I asked looking down at her.

"Crab's sound good. I'm Ok with it if you are."

"Yeah, sounds good to me."

When she was finished her coffee, she jumped in the shower and dressed for the day. Today she wore a simple sun-dress that was white and had small sunflowers on it. The white sandals she wore were a nice accent to her outfit. When she was finished, I took her back to my place so I too could shower and change. I was hoping we would be alone but had no such luck as both Kyle and Weston were home for some reason and by the time I got downstairs Molly had also returned home. They were all chit chatting and catching up on the last couple of years. It seemed to me that it was natural looking and that she still seemed to belong here. Maybe she never should have left? The only one not overly happy looking was Molly. I caught her several times looking over at me. Was it too painful on her to see me with Sarah? We were not putting on a public display of affection or anything like that, but could the simple sight of Sarah hurt Molly as well?

By the time we decided to leave though it was a little before 2pm and as we walked out the door, I heard Kyle tell me not to worry about it. Meaning he would make sure no one said anything to Syd about Sarah's visit.

We had just enough time to get in a game of mini golf, so we stopped at an Ole Pro Minigolf place on the way back to the condo. She was pleased with herself having beaten me yet again. I was out of practice as Sydney and I rarely played miniature golf. Sarah apparently played often.

"Nope. Not since you David." She said as if having to defend herself. By the time we had finished it was time to head back for dinner. It had been a while since I had crabs and I had to agree with Sarah that they were indeed tasty. Dinner went by quickly though and the conversation stayed light over the course of the next two hours or so it took to eat. We did not have to explain or even say what time we had made it in by the night before. Maybe because she was now 22 and an adult? I do not know, but it never came up and so neither did the need to say anything of the night before.

We had decided to stay in for the night, maybe make it an earlier evening since we had been up so late the night before and we excused ourselves to the back balcony that overlooked the ocean. Sarah grabbed a bottle of wine and a couple of glasses and as we left the kitchen area I could once again see her mom smiling. After a glass each, she began to talk. Really talk. She opened up about the last two years, experiences at school, student teaching, where she got her teaching position, and of course her personal life as well.

Neither of us had brought up our love lives apart from each other, until now. This is when I had heard for the first time that she had been engaged. Had been was stressed, but it was also a recent had been. She told me about the final straw that caused her to cancel the wedding. She had started planning it, and hearing about this other guy that she had loved enough to say yes to a marriage proposal hurt me. I had no right to feel hurt, but I was. She had even told me about how she knew exactly what she needed to save in the next year in order to buy her own house. Unsure of the time, but knowing it was getting late, we moved from the balcony and into her bedroom. We laid on her bed facing each other, fully clothed though in case her parents decided to drop in on us.

"Oh my God Sarah. Your life is so in order." I said to her awe struck by the strides she had taken since we were last together. "I just decided what I think I want to do with my life and you're already buying houses and planning a wedding." I could not hide the distress in my voice as I looked over at her.

"Was. The key word being "was" planning a wedding." She said trying to ease my apprehension. She asked me to fill her in on the last two years as well. So, I did except for my attempted suicide. I told her about school, volleyball, and of course Sydney. She was happy for me that I had someone special in my life. It seemed genuine as well.

I knew I could never be happy knowing she had someone special in her life. It would hurt too much. At some point our eyes had gotten heavy, our hands had found each other's, and our words came to an end. With the lights still on to keep it innocent looking we had fallen asleep and at some point, in the night her mom had come in and turned off the light.

48

Saturday morning came and as I woke up, I could see Sarah was wrapped in my arms as we laid on top of the blankets of her bed and still fully clothed. I was not sure of the time, but I felt like it was mid-morning. I unwrapped myself from her arms without waking her and walked out into the condo's living room. Sarah's mom was in the kitchen cleaning up from breakfast as her dad was sitting on the balcony reading his newspaper.

"Good morning sunshine. Coffee?" She asked smiling over at me. I gave her my good morning greeting and waved to her father as well. I was told to go on and take Sarah her coffee as well, so I did. When I walked into the room once again, I could see that she was no longer clothed in the clothes she wore from last night but had put on the silky blue nighty that she had worn back on Thursday morning when I had picked her up. Her eyes were closed though.

"Come lay with me." She beckoned to me extending her hand out to me. I took it willingly and laid next to her. Quietly I allowed my hand to caress her body as gently as I could stirring feelings in both her and me. Occasionally I would allow my hand to stop to explore some of the more delicate areas of her body and when I would soft gentle sighs would escape her mouth.

"Don't you dare stop David" Her eyes were barely open as she seemed completely lost in the moment.

"What about your parents?"

"I don't care about them at the moment. We can be really quiet."

"The bed will make noise" I tried to say in protest. She stood, made her way to the front of the bed, and threw a blanket on the floor laying on top of it.

"Now get over here!" She whispered in a quiet yet demanding voice. I did as I was asked and went straight for her.

We did not speak again until afterwards when we heard the front door closing. We spent the rest of the day together relaxing at the beach. She had wanted to go as it was going to be her last day to do so for a while. Her parents had left a note telling us to have a good day and that it was going to be dinner at The Bonfire tonight if we wanted to join. I suggested to Sarah that she do dinner with her parents tonight since she had yet to spend any time with them by herself and that I would meet her at 9pm at The Ocean Club.

A mutual friend of ours was a bartender there and I knew Brian would love to see her. She reluctantly agreed. Sitting on the beach in some beach chairs, looking out into the water, holding hands, I was completely lost in thought. I was scared. We still had not talked about what the last few days and nights had meant for us and I was not sure if that was intentional or not. I had so many thoughts running through my head both good and bad and I feared what this could mean.

"Be still David. We have all the time in the world to figure things out" she said as if feeling my mood change. She always knew. I squeezed her hand tighter in reassurance. We kept the talk light after that not wanting to ruin our last precious moments at the beach together. Reality would set in tomorrow and it was in that last couple of hours together that I knew what I had to do, and I once again started the process of memorizing every detail of her I could.

I walked her back to the front door of the condo and kissed her goodbye. She reminded me about meeting her later at the Ocean Club and I told her how I could not wait to see her later. We kissed again and again only separated when the door had forced us to drop hands. I walked back down the stairs and heard Sarah call down from the balcony.

"David!" I looked up at her smiling. She had the sundress on over her bikini but this time she was in bare feet and her hair had been let down out of its ponytail. Perfect I thought. Absolutely Perfect.

"Yes Sarah?"

"I love you. Truly and completely. I have always loved you." The tone of her voice was one of absolute conviction with no doubt in it at all. There was a hint of sadness in her voice as if she knew something was wrong. She always knew, even before I ever did.

"There has never been another Sarah and I feel as if there never will be. You are the love of my life and it is my greatest joy to have ever met you." I equaled her sincerity, and sadness.

"I will see you tonight." She said it as if wanting to make sure I would remember.

"Yes. Goodbye Sarah." I took one last look of her, saw her hair and dress flutter a little in the breeze, saw her beautiful blue eyes, and the smile on her face, then turned and walked away knowing what must be done. I once again knew how to love her.

49

I was so sad when I walked through the door to my place. I was ready to cry once again. I knew what I had to do, and I knew it would crush us both. I knew that in order for Sarah and me to have a real chance of working out one of two things would need to happen. Either she would have to uproot her life and move to the beach, which seemed an utterly selfish thing to ask of her, or I would have to move home to her. That was the more realistic thing to do but would still delay her life years for me to catch up to her and where she is in life. Both of those choices seemed so unfair to ask of her, both seemed so very selfish of me to ask. I concluded the best thing I could do for Sarah, the best way I could love her and give her the best shot at a great life was to let her go. Let her go and hope the douche bag she had been engaged to could patch things up and make her happy.

The knowledge of what I had to do was overwhelming to me and I could not contain my sadness any longer and as I walked in through the door of my house, I did not even bother saying hello to my roommates and made my way up to my room. I needed to be alone. I was too overwhelmed to fake happiness tonight and my friends would see the pain I was in and would know something was wrong. There was no way I would be able to explain this. I took the phone off the hook around 9pm and about that time Sydney finally came upstairs and sat next to me. I could see she was crying as well. She hugged me though and we both cried together.

"I'm so sorry" I sobbed into her shoulder.

"I'm sorry for you" She replied. I separated from her and gave her a quizzical look.

"Jesus David, you smell like her. I'd recognize that scent anywhere. It's the same way you smelled when you were late picking me up that day for volleyball. I know you've been with her and by the way you are acting I have a rather good idea as to what is happening tonight."

Again, I gave her another quizzical look. She pointed at the phone that I had taken off the receiver in order give a busy signal to anyone that calls.

"You are standing her up, aren't you?" I could only nod as confirmation. Another sob left my body and Sydney held me once again. "Why not tell her in person?"

"Because it has to hurt her enough to move on from me completely, forget about me if she can, there can be no doubt in her mind and the thought of what it will do to her is killing me and if I am being totally honest, the idea of losing her forever is almost unbearable for me." Sydney sat silently next to me still holding me when needed. The thought occurred to me that this must be destroying Sydney as well.

On one hand she knew that the one person who she was never able to live up to would no longer be an issue, but at the same time the knowledge that her boyfriend had once again ran back to that person without a single thought about her had to be devastating.

"I am so sorry Syd. I should have let sleeping dogs lie." She held me a little tighter but did not answer me. I tried to tell her how it all happened, but she would interrupt me and told me she did not want to know. Ever. We sat in silence until 11pm and knew we had to put the phone back on the hook. The call came a little before midnight.

"Answer it" Sydney demanded wanting me to do what needed to be done. I picked up the phone and said hello. My voice came out hoarse.

"Hello"

"What the fuck was that? Why the fuck would you stand me up like that?" Sarah's voice was hot with anger. I could hear hatred in it as well.

"I'm sorry" I had no words to tell her other than a standard apology.

"Sorry? Sorry? What kind of answer is that?"

"Sarah, the last few days were fun."

"Fun?" She said yelling into the phone. "It was fun? I bare my heart and soul to you and your thoughts were that it was fun?"

"Look Sarah, Yes. It was great seeing you again, but I have a girlfriend and I"

"Don't ever talk to me again! Ever!" she yelled into the phone interrupting me. I heard the click of the phone and then the dial tone signaling that she had hung up on me. Tears welled up inside me and rolled down my face. Sydney hugged me once again tightly.

"Goodbye Sarah, Goodbye" I cried into the phone then hung up the line. As Sydney held me and tried her best to console me, I thought about how amazing she was. She was as perfect as Sarah. Almost. And as I laid there crying, I thought about the last few days. All the emotions that were shared, the passion we felt, the intimacy that we confessed we have only ever had with each other, her beating me in the race at the Fun House and in mini golf, ice cream, the boardwalk, making love at the beach, laying in complete silence, and a smile returned to my face. I would never love another like her, but I had done the best thing I could for her. I had set her free once again.

A thought crossed my mind, could two people as spiritually, emotionally, mentally, and physically connected as we were, if there truly was something like a soul mate, and we had both agreed that we knew we were that to each other, could it or would it ever truly be over for us? That single thought made me smile. I do not know the answer to that question. Maybe someday in the future our paths would cross again, but for now I was glad that I had taken the time to study her face, to learn her body, to memorize the sound of her laugh, so that I could remember her so completely. And up until the last few heartbreaking hours I had once again had those perfect moments in my life, and I would forever be grateful for them and for the last three plus days with the love of my life Sarah Fulton. If I were to ever be granted one more wish, I hope that some day I will be able to explain to Sarah why I did what I did. So that she would know it was out of love for her that I had to let her go and that maybe, just maybe, she would be able to forgive me for breaking her heart, and mine as well.

50

I felt terrible. The rest of the summer was horrible in every way possible. Sarah was gone. My job was stressful. Sydney was, well, about as perfect as she could be considering, but I knew that episode with Sarah was terribly hurtful to her and I feared there was no recovering from it. She tried; God love her she tried to get past it, but it ate away at her like cancer. She would have good days and it seemed like we were going to get through it, but when the bad days would come, they were difficult to handle, and I was not emotionally strong enough for both of us and whereas Sydney had been before she now closed herself off during those times focusing on herself. Who could blame her? I had to be patient and remain hopeful. I tried to love her the best I could, but that day in August I broke two hearts and I too had days where I could not be what Sydney needed and for the first time, I dreaded the fall and winter months.

Sydney had gone back to school again, and although it was part time there were times where she would stay back home for a week straight. When I would ask when she was coming back, she would reply that she was not sure, she needed time, and then remind me that I broke her heart and she was trying her best, but...... I understood. Not two hearts, but three.

Kyle decided to head home for a while feeling the need to do better at school. He did not say one way or the other, but we all felt a girl had something to do with it. I hoped that was the case. When Kyle was in a relationship, he seemed much happier than when he was playing his alphabet game. A companion, long term companion, was good for him. He was more motivated, at least to me it seemed that way.

Weston did stay for the fall and Molly was around almost full time. She worked, she cleaned, she cooked, she did her part, but she too was on the sullen side. Our traditional Friday night dinners were not the same. They were no longer something to look forward to and by Thanksgiving they seemed to drift away becoming the rarity rather than the norm. I began to feel like that not only did I possibly destroy things with Syd, but the entire house. It did not feel like a home anymore and I could see that even Weston's normally overly perky attitude was starting to wane as well.

I missed Sydney. I missed her love, and I finally understood what Kristy had tried to tell me so long ago, I did love Sydney just in a different way. I feared the realization was too late. I am an emotionally needy person though and where Sydney, rightfully so, was withholding and guarding herself, there was one person I knew would be more than willing to connect with me, and the night of Thanksgiving I made a call that I knew eventually may cause great harm to everyone, but I did not care.

"Hello?" Molly said into the phone. Sydney had decided to travel with her parents for the holiday weekend. I did not mind. Things were tense between us. I tried, as best as I could, to make up for things but I was failing miserably. I needed love too. I have always craved closeness and affection and I missed that now.

"Hey. What are you doing?" I asked her somewhat seductively. It was time to see if I still could be the closer I once was. Maybe do Kyle proud?

"Just sitting her by myself. What are you up to?"

"Pretty much the same. I was wondering if you wanted some company?" I asked knowing the answer. Weston had also gone out of town for the weekend choosing to go to Austin to see some friends there. I was hoping she might seize the chance to be alone for the weekend.

"I don't get it. What are you asking me?" She was apparently confused and not catching my hint at a weekend alone together.

"I'm saying to come spend the weekend with me." She did not answer right away so I continued hoping to convince her. "Look, I know Weston is gone for the weekend, so is Sydney. I'm here alone, and you're there alone, why should we both have to be alone when we can spend the weekend together? Just the two of us." I could tell she was thinking about it. "Molly, it will be fun. No one needs to know. Just you and I until they get back."

"David." her voice was unsure sounding. I could tell she wanted to but was uneasy about it to say the least. "What are you expecting to happen?" She asked me. A little concern had found its way into her voice.

"Nothing you don't want and everything you do. You lead. You decide. I would just like your company for the next few days." I responded almost pleading with her. I was wondering if I sounded a little too much like Weston. After a few moments of silence, she finally answered.

"Ok. I'll leave now. Bye." The phone went silent. It was a two-and-a-half-hour drive from Bowie where her parents lived, she was here with me in under two.

51

I was looking forward to spending time with her. I always knew I leaned slightly co-dependent. I struggled with loneliness and where Sydney, for reasons that were obviously my fault, could not be there for me I still needed someone who could. Why not Molly? Part of me understood well how wrong this was, not just because of Sydney, but Weston too. I was not exactly going to steal his girlfriend, just kind of borrow her for a bit. Still despicable I know, but I knew I would feel better and that was all that mattered to me. At least for the moment. At least for the weekend. When I heard her car pull up, I had just hopped out of the shower. She must have been flying as she was a full thirty minutes earlier then what the trip would normally take. I wrapped a towel around my waist and went to greet her.

"Hey" I said opening the door for her. She looked me up and down and I could not gauge her mood. I did not know her well enough to tell how she was feeling but she seemed somewhat serious.

"Oh dear God. Really? A towel only?" she replied smiling slyly. I had not thought about my attire as anything to be worried about. She has seen me in just a towel before.

"I just got out of the shower. You got here quickly." I said trying to defend myself against anything planned by me and my current choice of covering.

She herself was dressed in a little black cotton miniskirt that fit loosely on her and a simple white Nike sweatshirt with a black swoosh. Comfortable and yet desirable as well. She pushed me back through the door and backed me up all the way to the couch in the living room. She pushed me onto the couch and then sat down on me straddling me. Looking into my eyes she spoke again.

"You knew exactly what would happen this weekend" and then she kissed me, and I felt better.

Sex with Molly was different. Not loving, or tender, but still passionate enough. Kind of raw. More physical than emotional and yet she was ok with it. I let Molly dictate it. If she kissed me, I'd kiss her back. If she pulled the back of my hair or gripped my neck, I would squeeze her tighter. If she rocked her body at a faster pace than I would as well. I was a complimentary partner to whatever she needed in the moment and when she finally collapsed on me panting, I stayed still and allowed her to regain herself. No words though had been spoken since the front door. After she had caught her breath and brushed away her hair from her face she looked over and smiled.

"Wow." She was still trying to catch her breath a little and when I looked over at her I saw her attempting to blow stray hairs away from her face.

"Is that a good wow?" I asked looking for reassurance.

"That was different, but in a good way." I frowned a little not sure I was liking her assessment.

"No. No. No. Simply different from what I'm used to with Weston" still I frowned then she added "But in a good way. A really really good way." Now I was smiling. I had always assumed I was better than Weston but now I was curious as to how or why.

"How so?" I asked. I needed to know. She sat up and laid her head on my shoulder draping her arm across my chest and stomach.

"Well for one thing you are quiet where he never shuts up. He's always smiling or giggling like he's surprised he's actually doing it. Like a kid might who just got away with stealing a cookie from a cookie jar without getting caught. I don't know how to explain it. Childish like maybe?" That sounded like how I pictured him to be like. "He also tries to dirty talk way too much. Kind of a turn off to me." she imitated his voice then said "Oh baby you know you like that don't you. I said don't you." I could not help but laugh at that. I could see him do that as well.

"I'm thinking of course I like it, or I would stop, but you, you were so quiet. I wasn't sure if I was living up to what you're used to, so I felt like I needed to do more kind of thing." I kissed the top of her head. "But then when it did finally end, I got the feeling like I must have done ok."

"You were great. Thank you for that." I said trying to re-assure her.

"I also liked that you were ok with me being in control. Weston tends to pound away like he thinks he's a porn star." I laughed. "It's not funny." She said lifting her head off me to scold me. I stopped laughing. "And it definitely isn't romantic" She laid her head back down "Or loving."

She missed romance. She missed love. I did not feel that this had been romantic or loving though. I thought maybe she did because my allowing her to do what she had wanted was to her the loving thing? I did not know, but she was happy, so I fig-ured that was a good thing.

We sat there on the couch for the rest of the evening only moving to answer the door for the pizza we ordered. We started a fire, turned the TV on and watched the movie Congo, and sometime after midnight we both fell asleep.

52

The rest of the weekend went much the same. Wake up, have sex, eat, watch a movie, have sex again, eat, maybe walk the beach, then sleep in my room together. We both took turns calling our significant others. It was easier to call them and get it out of the way rather than they call us. Molly had told Weston that she was back home so better to call him rather than him try to get her at home since she was not there. Her conversations lasted much longer than mine and both of us would attempt to distract the other while they were on the phone encouraging a quicker call. It was a fun weekend all in all and I was glad that she had agreed to come.

I had noticed that I had seen her smile more in the last three days than the entirety of the last three months. She seemed happy and I was glad I had been a part of her happiness. When she heard a car pull up into our little gravel parking area she leaned over and gave me one last quick kiss and thanked me for a great weekend. She left me on the couch and took a place in the love seat next to the couch as Weston walked through the door.

"Molls? Guess who's home baby?" Weston said extending the y. He was smiling ear to ear and looked happy to be back. Molly looked at me after his cheesy way of saying baby as if saying "See? A child?" I smiled at her in return. Weston came in, waved his hello to me, gave Molly a kiss on her head, then told us he would be back because flying always gave him the runs. I laughed. Molly did not.

Once we heard the bathroom door closing, she hurriedly came back over to me and assumed her Thursday night position.

"Molly, what are you doing?" I asked in between her kisses. "He's right upstairs." I tried to say thinking it would get her to stop.

"He always takes a quick shower after using the bathroom like that. You've got ten minutes. I challenge you to complete this in ten minutes" she said longingly. I looked at her eyes judging her resolve. Was she really willing to risk this? I could see she was.

"Challenge accepted."

Molly knew Weston well. 5 minutes later the toilet flushed, and the shower turned on. At the nine-minute mark we both finished what needed to be finished and holding each other afterwards in that euphoric state our eyes only opened when the water turned off.

"Perfect timing" she said as we both laughed a little with her still sitting on top of me.

"Yes, it was. Except for the front door being left open." A voice said from kitchen that looks into the living room. We both turned our heads to see that at some point Kyle had come home. I was not expecting him since he is normally only here for the weekend and since it is Sunday night, I figured he would not be coming since this is when he normally leaves. Molly quickly jumped off me, grabbed her clothes, and ran up the stairs and into Weston's room closing and locking the door behind her. Kyle got that stupid huge grin on his face.

"How long have you been there?" I asked a little heated with his surprise entrance.

"Long enough. Good finish by the way. Kissing the base of her neck at the end, smooth. I'll have to try that." I looked away from him. "Jesus David, I thought you told me the one time only back in June. And that was just a pity kiss! This though, this crosses some major lines." He said then he added "even for you" as if emphasizing the point.

"It was not a pity kiss" I said feeling the need to defend what happened in June. It was not pity. I had really enjoyed myself, but it was not love either. So, what was it? Kyle stared at me as if expecting more information than what had been given.

"Look. I know this is wrong." I started.

"On so many levels" he said interrupting me.

"On so many levels. Something about it makes me feel good though."

"Oh. I get it. I try to have as much sex as I can too." He replied thinking that I was referring to the physical and not the emotional feelings.

"No. That's not it. I mean yeah that too, but I mean emotionally. She's good for me right now. It feels good to be wanted."

"Oh. I get that too! You can get that from another girl though. Does it really have to be Weston's girlfriend? And if Syd isn't doing it for you right now than why not put that girl out of her misery? Poor thing has been waiting on you fulfilling your promise ring deal for two plus years! Make good or let her go." He was right. I knew he was right.

I knew why this was going on with Molly though. I understood how she felt and if I could take back not showing up for dinner last August with Sarah I would, but I can't and so now I am trying to make Molly feel a little bit better by being with her, even if it is just for a few moments because if I could have just a few moments with Sarah right now I would take them and treasure them.

Weston made his way down the stairs and into the living room and Kyle turned away from me and made like he was looking for something to eat.

"Where's Molly" Weston asked buttoning up his Hawaiian print shirt.

"She went upstairs." Kyle answered with his head still

buried in the refrigerator. "She mentioned something about cramps, PMS, something like that." I smiled. Even as pissed at me as he is he was still covering for me. No way Weston would try to fool around with her tonight if he thought she was having her cycle. Weston looked up at the ceiling and had a look on his face as if he were counting days.

"Seems early to me. Damn. I raced back here from the airport too." Weston sat down on the couch and picked up the latest issue of Volleyball Monthly and began thumbing through its pages.

"I think I'll go upstairs and try calling Syd" I said. I was feeling a little guilty after my very brief conversation with Kyle. I went upstairs to my room, closed the door, climbed into bed, and turned the Tv on. Guilt would not allow me to call Sydney. Not guilt over this weekend, or because Molly was Weston's girlfriend, or because I was once again doing something that Sydney would not approve of, but because I kind of missed her, and by her, I mean Molly.

I wished she would cross the hall and come into my room. The guilt was because after this weekend there was more emotion there than should be, but I did not care because I liked it. It was exactly what I needed at the moment and damn everyone else's feelings.

1996

53

Weston had graduated from the University of Maryland in May. He had decided to have one more summer in the sun and would start putting his resume out hopeful for a career type job come Fall. If need be though he would move home earlier. We all understood. I could tell though that he was anxious and his time at the beach was not the fun relaxing time he wanted but rather time he felt he could be pounding the pavement instead. His relationship with Molly was on a slow steady downward spiral as well. I did not think it was entirely my fault, but I am sure our little interludes together did not help. I am sure it was hard on her to get over me and move on when the one you love is sleeping with you whenever he can. I hated myself over it at times. Not because of Weston or Sydney but because I knew it made things harder on Molly. She came down as often as she could, and I had made several trips back to her as well. Sometimes picking her up right after Weston had dropped her off at her house.

It was not always sex with us. Sometimes we would just go to the lake near my parents' house and sit on a blanket and talk while looking up at the stars. It was nice having her company and it was nice to feel wanted in return.

Kyle was his normal happy self. In March though his

father had told us that he had been diagnosed with Congestive Heart Failure and that it was terminal. Doctors had given him maybe two years to live. Kyle would go home often but his dad had insisted he live his life and stay at the beach for the summer. So, Kyle did, but I knew his days here were numbered as well.

In May Sydney had finished her junior year at UMBC and I could tell she was thinking about future stuff. The promise ring specifically. In two and a half years what had I really done to make this a reality for her? Not much. Sure, I had taken a few classes, but I was at least two plus years at full time from graduating. It would be easy to understand why someone would think I should be further along.

My job was still the same and all though I was now managing my own store it was not exactly a job that could support a family. I knew too that beach volleyball was never going to be a full-time career where I could make a decent living as well. In Sydney's opinion I should think of it as just a hobby at this point. She was right.

I wish I could say that was a onetime thing with Molly, but it was not. I wish I could say that things had gotten better with Sydney, but they have not. I wish I could say that the excitement of living at the beach with the people closest to me had returned, but that too seemed gone forever. I will always love the beach and I will always cherish the memories that were made while living here, but the luster of being here had worn off on us all. I knew, if no one else did, why we were all feeling as if our time here together was ending. We were all getting older and yet we were all stagnant in life. None of us were where we thought we would be at twenty-five years old and time was beginning to feel like it was against us all. People we knew our age were in their careers, getting married, having kids, and buying houses. Adulting, and we were starting to feel guilty about not being in that same place in life.

Weston was the closest and stood the best chance of

making it happen but as I said earlier, he was feeling anxious about it. This understanding of where we all were in life hit me the hardest. I felt like a bum and to me it felt like the world was crashing in around me. I had trouble focusing on my job, volleyball became a chore rather than fun, the thought of how long school was going to take was dreadful to me and made me not want to go, my relationship with the person who had loved me the most was crap and rather than fix it I was taking refuge in the arms of one of my best friends girlfriend and even that I knew was causing the one I was running to pain and suffering. I had not felt this terrible about life in an awfully long time. It felt unbearable and as I sank into those dark places that only I ever seem to have the ability to go it made things with Sydney even worse.

"David I can't do this anymore."

It was Saturday of Memorial Day weekend and Sydney had just gotten in town less than an hour ago. When she had walked in, I could tell she was not happy. Her eyes were swollen, and I could tell she had been crying.

"What are you talking about Syd?" I asked not understanding her comment. She took my hand in hers. I was not sure if it was for my benefit or hers.

"I mean, I'm done David. I've tried. I really have, but I just don't have it in me anymore." She took the promise ring off and placed it into my hand. I could only stare down at it.

"Why?" I asked. I knew why, but I could not think of anything better to say at the moment. She stood up in front of me then started to pace back and forth. It was what she did when she was starting to get angry. Fire entered her eyes. I probably should not have asked why.

"Why?" She said raising her voice. "Why?" Even louder this time. "Because I can't be with someone who doesn't love me the way I do them. Not anymore at least." She yelled. "Five years David! Five years I've been with you and I've lived in her shadow almost the entire time. You'll never love me the way you do her." She started to cry. "And that sucks because I did love you that way." I could only look at her. I had no words. She regained her composure a bit then went on with her reasoning.

"I don't know David. It's more than that. I just don't believe you love me at all. Maybe ever. I think you loved that I loved you and that I was there and loyal, but that isn't love." I hate how right she was. I could feel the darkness welling up inside of me. "What sucks is I got the worst part of you. I never got your best, I never got the best person you can be, the best of your love, your best effort in life, and yet I loved you anyway. She didn't though. And every single time you were broken into pieces I was the one to help you pick those pieces up." She was still pacing.

"I'm sorry" I muttered in almost a whisper.

"After last August though" She paused as if trying to find the right words to make sure I understood "I don't know. I've tried to get over it, but I just can't. Every time we kiss or more since then I just can't help but think of how you spent those three and a half days with her!"

"But Syd we"

"Don't you dare try to tell me nothing happened. Don't you dare attempt to lie to me like that." there was still so much anger in her voice. "I deserve better than lies." She did. She has always been nothing less than perfect with me. She came and knelt in front of me retaking my hands in hers.

"David. I think it would have been different if you had made any progress on the things you said you would. What that promise ring you gave me meant and stood for, but you haven't." Her voice was much calmer now and the fire had left her eyes.

"But I have. I'm back in school, I'm"

"No David. No." She interrupted me shaking her head. "Taking a class or two isn't accomplishing anything. Being content in your dead-end job isn't accomplishing anything. Not talking to a Doctor about your depressional issues isn't accomplishing anything. Bottom line is you are not doing anything to help yourself. I don't even feel like you are living anymore but rather just existing. You never finish anything. Especially if it gets tough."

"What?" I asked her confused of this new line of thinking.

"Volleyball, bowling, school, your job, your relationships. Every time something starts to get a little tough you shut down and quit. Every single time with every single thing." She stood back up and walked towards the stairs looking up them. "I can't have you drag me down with you David. I love you. I think I always will" she turned back to look at me "but after five years off and on, I need to focus on myself. I need to live."

"I'm sorry Sydney" I said choking down the tears.

"I forgive you David, but I need to go. I'm going to grab my things and then head home." She walked up the stairs and into our room. I thought about her words, about how badly I had treated her, and how good she has always been to me, and I knew what a horrible person I was. I laid down on the couch and began to weep silently.

Sydney came back down about thirty minutes later with her bag full of her stuff thrown over her shoulder. When she got to the front door she turned and looked back at me.

"Goodbye David. I hope you find the happiness that I couldn't give you. I will miss you." and then she walked out the door.

54

Sydney's leaving had hurt. More than I ever would have anticipated. She was the most faithful, caring, loving, and devoted person to me and I had never been able to return those feelings to her in the way I should have. I had always treated her with nothing more than complete selfishness. It was all about me and I knew it. I had spurned the one person who had always accepted me for who I was. It hurt not because my heart was broken, not like the way it had been with Sarah, but because if the one person who loved me for who I was was able to leave than I must be lower than shit at this point, or at least had become unlovable. That thought had hurt.

I had only sat there alone on the couch crying to myself that day for maybe ten minutes before Kristi, Kyle, and Weston made their way into the house. Sydney had called Kristi and she had flown in from California that same day. Sydney had called her to be here for me in case it went south quick. Even breaking up with me she showed nothing but love for me. Kyle and Weston were quiet allowing Kristi to handle the comforting this time. There was no such thought of suicide though, at least not directly. Indirectly was a different story. I had lost the ability to keep any kind of food down. I would eat and immediately my body would reject the food causing me to vomit uncontrollably. The doctors thought it was all in my head caused by my current state of depression. I was put on anti-depressants yet again.

I never liked those drugs. To me it seemed like they took away all ability to feel. I felt nothing. Sometimes it is better to hurt than to feel nothing. You lose what it means to be human when you lose the ability to feel emotions.

Volleyball I knew was over. I had tried to do a few tournaments, but my heart was not into it. The final realization happened when playing in a tournament in Dewey Beach, Delaware, I chose to go to work rather than play a tie breaker match. My partner was not happy, and that decision eventually ended our partnership.

Work was nothing but stress. I felt like I was there all the time. Managing a store meant being there and the time spent was time not thinking about life and that had its benefits as well. It was a slow lead up. The stress, the being lied to by ownership, the hours, and the fact that I knew this was not a career job.

So here I was. Twenty-five years old, living at the beach, not going to school currently, dead end job, and worst of all no girlfriend to speak of with no one even interested. I understood. The look of someone struggling with their life and deep depressional issues does not come off as attractive to the opposite sex. Even Molly had managed to separate herself from me. I am assuming I was not as loveable as I used to be in her eyes. Just one more person who loved me and now no longer does.

I had decided to reach out to the one person I thought could make me smile. I knew there was a chance she would not want to talk to me, but I decided to try and call her anyway. No harm in trying right? I started dialing and a smile had started to appear on my face. Sitting in my room on this Wednesday afternoon I was finally smiling. I heard a familiar voice answer on the fourth ring.

"Hello?" the voice said into the phone.

"Hi Mr. Fulton. Can I please speak to Sarah?" I said way to excitedly. There was silence for a few moments.

"I'm sorry who is this?" He asked back as if not knowing my voice.

"It's David Anderson Mr. Fulton." I answered back starting to feel a little uneasy. Did she not want to talk to me? Had she left instructions to not let me talk to her? Maybe she had bought a house like she was talking about? No, it was much worse than any of those possibilities.

"David, I don't think it's a good idea for you talk to her right now." He said sounding both confident and yet sad at the same time.

"Oh" was all I could say then thought to add "Can you tell her I tried calling please?" Again, silence before he answered.

"David, I don't think that's a good idea either." He still sounded so sad and then he said the words I'll never forget and that finally broke me.

"She's getting married on Saturday and I don't think it's such a good idea if you two talk." I was crushed. He was right though, and I knew what I had to say.

"No. You are right. I didn't know about the wedding."

"Thanks for understanding. Goodbye David." Then I heard the phone hang up. I was now lost for good. The only person I had ever truly loved was now out of my life for good. I had set her free last August, said goodbye to her then, but I had always felt like we would reconnect again like we always have, this time though, this time was truly for good. My heart sank with the thought.

I began to think of all the things she and I had done over the previous 8 years. Our first date, our first kiss, prom, holidays, her homecoming, trips to the beach, the parking lot at the college, mini golf, how competitive she was, my fascination with dunking her after we would kiss, her many trips to see me here, and at some point, it turned into thinking about her hair, her smile, and her beautiful blue eyes. Oh, how I loved when she would get that serious look in them, that look when I could see how she felt about me. Oh, how I wish I could see that look now.

Just. One. Last. Time.

I could not take it anymore. This was too hard to deal with. The load too heavy. My world had all crashed in around me and I could not handle this last goodbye.

55

"You can't live on grilled cheese forever. You're barely 135lbs now!" Kyle said looking down at me. I was praying at the porcelain altar in our bathroom. Fresh bandages covered my lower arms from my latest attempt at ending life. Sydney had told me I have issues finishing anything, I guess she was right. For as many times as I have tried to end my life you would think I would have gotten better at it by now. I looked up at Kyle and tried my best to reassure him that this too might pass in time.

"It's all I can keep down; I need to be able to eat something." It was true. 1996 had not been a kind year so far. Now in mid-August I had just been dealt a terrible blow. The worst thing imaginable. Worse than my off and on girlfriend of the last five years dumping me back at the end of May, worse than anything imaginable to most, it was the end of my life.

The doctors had said I was lucky. In their eyes maybe, but certainly not in mine, apparently once again someone had walked in at just the right time. I had already passed out when Weston and Molly found me and unlike Kyle, or Kristi, or even Sydney, Weston had called an ambulance. I spent the next week in a hospital both on a hold for the attempt and for the wounds to heal. Sure, the cuts would heal, but I knew my heart was forever dead.

The only good thing about the hospital was that I was so medicated I missed even knowing that Saturday had come and gone. Thank God for small blessings, I guess. What was I thinking? I knew there was no God.

Kyle and Weston would visit every day. The first time I

was aware enough to know they were there I asked only one thing. Did they know? Both had responded that they had not. I was shocked. I would have thought she might invite Weston maybe since she knew him from way back in High School. I guess she would have known Kyle for about the same amount of time though too so he might have gotten the invite as well. It did not matter. I was only curious if they knew and were just trying to protect me.

Kristi flew back once again. She would sit with me and read to me. I missed her in my life. She would remind me that she was only a phone call away. That thought though was never much comfort. I missed my friend. I missed going to her house. I missed our hangouts. I just missed her.

In early September I had had enough. It was Friday of Labor Day weekend and my boss, the owner's son, had lied to me for the last time. When I called him up to confront him about, he tried to blame someone else. So, I told him their keys would be in the store and that I was locking up and quitting. By noon, the whole staff had walked out as well leaving him to work the holiday weekend by himself.

Kyle, Weston, Molly and I had enjoyed doing nothing but what we wanted to do that weekend. It had been a long time since we had done nothing but what we wanted while living at the beach. I had been slowly killing myself for the last three months at this point with my issue of not being able to eat without getting sick. I had been unhappy for an exceptionally long time without realizing it, but sitting on the beach on Labor Day, I knew what I needed to do. With no job, not being enrolled in school, no girlfriend here to worry about I knew what I needed to do. I needed to end the escape I had made so long ago. Whereas the beach had been a savior to me it had also turned into an inescapable trap. I had been stuck, without realizing it, under the impression that I could only be happy here. I smiled a little as I made my announcement.

"I'm going home." I said while staring out into the ocean. The three of them looked at me as if judging my seriousness. They must have seen that I was.

"I'll go with you." Kyle said smiling as well.

"Yeah. It's time." Weston said adding his thoughts into the conversation. Molly only looked at the water.

"I need to get out of here before I'm lost here forever." I told them sifting some sand through my hands.

"When?" Kyle asked.

"Tomorrow?" I answered back wondering if that was too soon. They all smiled as if waiting a lifetime for me to come to this conclusion.

"I mean it's not like we can't come back on weekends. We have the lease through January 13th." Kyle stated as if trying to make me feel better about the decision. He did not need to. I nodded my agreeance.

Weston grabbed all our hands and forced us to stand up while looking out to the water. The sky was turning orange with hints of purple as the sun went down behind us.

"It was a good run fellas. It was a good run." We all wrapped an arm around the person next to us on either side and stood there in silence for what seemed like a lifetime lost in our own memories. I thought of surfing, volleyball, my other friends that lived here, my favorite surf shop, the different places we had rented, friends that had come down to visit, mini golf, real golf with the guys, the boardwalk, Dina, Eric, Brent and others that had made their way here for visits. I thought a lot about Sydney, Molly, and especially Kyle, Weston, and Kristi. I thought about how I will always remember our Friday night dinners, and the fun things we would do after. The stupid video games, and parties. How I found out about Kyle and Kristi, and their food fights. And of course, I thought about Sarah. I started to cry a little and the arms around me gripped me tighter as if worried I would crumble.

"No guys. I'm happy. At least in this moment I am happy."

We stayed like that until the sky turned black. The Ferris Wheel down the way had its lights on and at that we knew it was time to go. We turned back to the water one last time.

"God, I love it here" Weston stated one last time sighing a little.

"Me too Weston, me too" I agreed.

Then in unison we all turned around and headed up the beach, away from the water, and back towards the car, heading to our new goals, our new lives. Sure, I was apprehensive and still a minor setback from jumping off a ledge, but there was something else too, hope. Just as the beach had given me hope so long ago now leaving it was also giving me hope. Hope of the possibility of bettering ourselves. Hope of a future. Hope of living and maybe, just maybe, happiness.

Later

56

"What happened after the beach?" I thought about what all I could tell her, how much to divulge. Sharing my past before a time that she knew of was one thing but admitting feelings of the more recent without possibly hurting hers was a little more difficult.

"Well Lindsey you know most of the rest. I moved home from the beach and met your mother. You know how that worked out." I tried to be tactful in my answer.

Lindsey, my beautiful youngest daughter, who up until recently I had always believed to be a happy soul, had just spent the better part of my weekend with her listening to my history of struggling with depression. She had recently discussed with her mother and I about her own struggles, her own thoughts of suicide, her own feelings of loneliness, and her mom had thought I might be able to understand her feelings on a level that she could not.

Lindsey was not just the youngest of my daughters, but the tallest as well. She had won the genetic lottery when it came to getting the best traits from her mother and me. She was tall

THE ENDLESS SUMMERS OF GOODBYES

at 5'11 though her basketball stat sheet would list her at 6'1, and athletic. All arms and legs when she was younger, now at 18 the rest of her body had caught up. Her blonde hair and brown eyes offset the fact that she had my nose, but if you asked her, she would say that she makes the nose look good. She was quick witted, and her sense of humor was fabulous. Her smile could light up the darkest of places and it was infectious. If ever there was a light in the world, it was my daughter Lindsey.

Do not get me wrong, all three of my daughters were beautiful. Each in their own unique way. Like their mom, all three were extremely smart and school came easy to them. When they were younger and would do something less than intelligent, I would tease them and say "Aw, it's a good thing you are pretty." If one would get into trouble, I would look at the other and say to her "This is why you are my favorite." To this day any card I get, or gift, text, whatever, is always signed "Your favorite."

Lindsey was the quietest of the three growing up, choosing to keep to herself most often. Once she got to the age of 12 though that changed quickly, and she soon seemed to have the largest personality of the three. It was hard for me to be sad around her as her laughter and personality would instantly lift my mood.

It was disheartening to hear that she struggled so deeply with depression. It was hard on me to think the apple had not fallen that far from the tree. Part of me could not see it in her, and then I remembered the mask I wore to others as well and I knew the truth of what she was feeling.

"So, you continued to struggle with depression issues back then?" She asked wanting more details. I decided I would be honest with her rather than sugar coat it.

"Well, meeting your mom helped. After about six months or so I was able to eat again."

"Go on." She said wanting to hear more.

"You know it already. We got married in 1998. Jules was born in end of '99. We moved to Colorado in '08. Separated in 2010." I kept things factual and without much emotion. She was listening intently while eating the frozen yogurt I had bought her.

"Why didn't you and mommy work out?" She asked me. Being that it was 2019 now a long time had passed since the last time I had thought about this and I will be honest, I do not remember what caused the final decision to end things.

"We were just too different Lindsey. Your mom is a great woman. A great mother. A great person in general. We just were not good together. I won't ever say anything bad about your mom. It simply did not work." She kept eating her yogurt, so I kept going. "Look Lindsey, the truth is your mom got me to do a lot of things I am not sure I ever would have done without her. I finished college, got real jobs in my field of study, helped me enjoy things like volleyball again, helped me find faith, she gave me a view of life that was different from my own. As you have heard me say though, I have struggled with a self-destructive nature my whole life. I have this dark side that I must manage, and I don't always accomplish that well. I am sure that played a huge role in why your mom and I did not work out. I don't know if I ever told her this or not, but I am sorry for the things that happened along the way. Maybe one day I will, and hopefully, she will be in a place where I can say that to her."

"So, even now you struggle?" She asked curious about my issues.

"Yes Lindsey. Let's see, after your mom and I split a slept in my car for two years because I couldn't afford a place. Part of that was defiance though too since your mom expected me to get a place." She looked over at me. "See? Self-destructive." I added.

"What else?"

"Well, for about a six-year period I was back to drinking

a bunch on the weekends." She looked shocked at this. "I didn't care anymore Lindsey, I wanted to live again, and I never drank on weekends I had you and your sister." She seemed somewhat relieved by that.

"You've heard me say that I hate Colorado. It's tough being a water person and being a 4-hour flight to the nearest ocean. Tough being so far away from Ohio as well. Not that moving here caused your mom and I to split, but it sure did not help either."

"The fact is Lindsey, the only thing that has kept me here for the last 8 years has been you and your sisters. Once you head off to college I will most likely move back."

"I'm not a fan either" She admitted. "I would like to be back on the east coast one day as well." She took another bite of her frozen yogurt. "How do you deal with it now? Do you feel better at all?"

"Sure, I do. I mean there are bad days, but I can go years now without feeling so down that I wonder if I can get back up. "

"Really?" She asked seeming hopeful.

"Yes! Absolutely. When Pops died three years ago, I was sad, but I managed without incident. I try my best now when these things happen, that I know could trigger me, to choose life. I focus on the good things rather than the negative. All issues are fixable, maybe not the way I want or expect, but with time I know things will get better. I choose life."

"Like what? What was fixed in a way that you didn't want?" She asked me curious of an example.

"Easy. Being married to your mom. No one gets married expecting to get divorced. No one. And I certainly didn't want things to end. They did though, and look how much happier everyone is? Things worked out."

"I understand." She said shaking her head. She seemed happier to me then when I first started the story. Since it was the stereotypical day in Denver with sunny skies and 75 degrees in early May, we decided to walk around Cheesman Park until I would need to drop her back off at her mom's house. She laughed a little thinking back on the story I had been telling her.

"I can't believe you thought it was easier to treat girls like crap rather then break up with them." I laughed at her comment. "I know you changed their names, but do I know any of those people?"

"Lindsey, I would not tell you if you did." I answered smiling at her.

"That sounds like a yes!" I laughed. "What? You would have said no if I did not know them." Dang her cleverness I thought to myself.

"Think what you want child." I said trying to play it off. Another thought came to her.

"Does mom know any of them?" She asked eagerly. I smiled. Better to stick to the truth I decided.

"Yes. At least a couple of them. I don't remember if I ever mentioned the girls in my life back then, but she knows some of the things I told you and a few of the guys as well." We continued to walk the exterior gravel path that circles the park. I loved Cheesman Park. It boasted maybe the best flower garden in the Parks and Rec system and had a separate rose garden as well. The trees were huge shade trees but there was plenty of open grassy areas to do different activities too. Lindsey once again broke the silence.

"Have you ever talked to any of the people from your past recently?" I smiled at her question before answering.

"Sydney contacted me a couple of years ago."

"Really?" She asked excitedly. "How did that go?"

"It went great!"

"What did you say to her?" She asked wanting details.

THE ENDLESS SUMMERS OF GOODBYES

"She sent me a friend request on Facebook. I accepted and then immediately sent her a long lengthy apology for how I treated her all those years ago."

"You did?" I could tell by her tone that she did not think I would do such a thing. I looked over at her as we continued our walk.

"Yes. I did. I had always felt awful about her. She was so sweet to me and I was awful to her."

"No argument there Dad." She said muttering a little. I looked back over at her again and she laughed. "What? You were horrible to her."

"I agree. Anyways. I apologized to her as best as I could. I told her how I have felt so bad about it over the last 20 years plus that I knew if I ever had the chance, I needed to make it right as best as I could."

"What did she say? What did she do?" She was enjoying this little update I could tell.

"I mean, she's Sydney. She did exactly what the person I described to you would do, she told me that no apology was needed but thanked me anyway."

"What?" Lindsey was in shock. "You were so bad though." I looked over at her again. It kind of stinks hearing my daughters' views of my previous relationships. Even if she was right. "So, how is she?"

"She is great! She is married, has a daughter about your age, the guy she is married to is a huge Ohio State fan, so I know he is a great guy, all in all she is awesome."

"Let's face it, after you it would have had to have gotten better." She said amused with herself.

"Easy there Linds. Your track record isn't so great either with your relationships." I teased her back.

"I am your daughter." She fired back. I smiled. Yes. Yes,

you are.

"What about the others? Do you still talk to them?" She asked. So curious this one is.

"Well, I still talk to Kristi. I try to see her every time I am back home." She looked over at me as if trying to think if she would know who Kristi was in real life. "You would have been a baby the last time you would have seen her." I said to her answering her silent question. "Kristi will always be a great friend. She is still married and incredibly happy."

"What about Weston, is he as funny as you made him sound?" I laughed at her question.

"Weston is great. Kyle needs a new hobby as he keeps having kids. Let's see who else?" I thought about everything we had talked about then continued "I guess that's it. The main ones I still see or talk to regularly."

"And Sarah?" She asked smiling at me.

"I have not spoken to Sarah since that night on the phone after standing her up."

"Did you ever look her up?" She asked genuinely interested. "And why would you love her enough to let her go? No girl wants that. Why not love her enough to do what is necessary to keep her love?"

"All good questions. I mean, sure I tried to look her up. I have no idea what her last name is now, but I tried her maiden name a couple of times. Just to see if she popped up. Nothing. She's pretty much disappeared as far as I know." She seemed a little disappointed by this. "As far as the other question goes" I sighed before answering her then tried my best to explain it. "I don't know. I honestly thought what I did was in her best interests. Looking back on it now, I should have shown up. I should have fought for her. I should have done what was needed, and I regret not showing up more than you could possibly ever know."

"All your issues seemed to be at their worst when it came

to relationships or is that how you portrayed it?" This child of mine is too perceptive. She does not miss a thing.

"There were plenty of things that fed my depression back then. Like Jack's brother dying just after your sister was born. Justin had passed away a few years before that while I was living at the beach. '96 was a terrible year, right after we moved home 6 weeks later Kyle's dad passed away. There were always other things that helped push me over the edge, but it was my personal relationships that would suffer the most. If there is one thing I have learned Lindsey, it is to get your mind right first before trying to be with someone. Don't make your happiness their responsibility. Choose life on your own."

We made our way back to the car and started the drive back to her house. I was alone in my thoughts, concerned for the well being of my daughter. I do not know if sharing my story with her has helped her at all, but I was praying it had. Thinking back to when I was younger would I have been receptive to my parents had they offered their help? What was I thinking? They did try and help, I had not realized it back then. The AA meetings, talks with the priest, those were attempts at getting me help. Would I have responded differently though to a more personal kind of help? I do not know. Maybe.

"Do you still struggle?" She asked while looking out at the foothills of the Rockies.

"Yes Lindsey, but not to the point I did when I was your age." I thought of a good thing for her and said, "And you are handling this much better than I was at your age."

"How so?" She looked over at me as my comment had clearly gotten her attention.

"First off, you told us. You asked for help. And you haven't tried anything yet right? Just thoughts?" She nodded her agreement. "See? Better than I had at this point. You are way ahead of where I was." She smiled at the thought.

"Dad, you should write about this."

"What?" I asked her unclear of what she meant.

"Write about your story, your issues, it could be thera-peutic. At least that's what my counselors say." I thought about this for a moment. It could be fun. A father daughter bonding experience.

"Ok, but you need to talk to me when you are feeling down. Call me when you are at your lowest. If you agree to that, I'll write."

She smiled as we got to her front door, and then she hugged me.

"Agreed."

57

"Dad! You can't release it yet. It should be perfect!" Lindsey told me wanting me to wait rather than rush the book before it was ready.

"Lindsey, I don't care anymore. I am over book 1. I need to finish book 2. I have put enough time into Be Still, Enjoy the Silence. I am releasing it. If there are errors, then there are errors. I never started this to make money or for people to buy it. I just want the ability to print it off and it look like a real book." I said frustrated.

It was true, writing the first book had been one of the toughest things I had ever done, but I finished it and in 2021 I had almost finished the second one as well. It was time to switch focuses. Lindsey was doing much better, and we were all happier for it. She has her bad times, but she seems happier. Maybe, like myself, she had gotten better at hiding how she was feeling from everyone else, but Lindsey had already been able to do that before admitting to us her struggles. As a father, I was praying that she was feeling better and not faking it to the rest of us.

"What is the title of the second one?" She asked me knowing there was no point in arguing the release of the first one. I know I am no Mark Twain. I just want to be able to print the damn thing off.

"Help me name it? The choices are Goodbyes Never End Well, or the one I like is The Endless Summers of Goodbyes."

"I like that one Dad, The Endless Summers of Goodbyes. It is so real for your story."

"So do I Lindsey. I think I'll go with that." There was

silence for a while. Neither of us knowing what to say. I knew she was busy at school. She went to a small school in Ohio for basketball and even though we were talking regularly, and she was getting the help she needed, it was hard knowing she was so far away from everyone. We all feared when she left knowing her struggles, but we had formed a plan, or I should say her mom had, and that plan involving the school, her coaches, doctors, etc. seemed to be working for her. I hoped my conversations helped her as well.

"You miss her, don't you?" She asked me in a deeply solemn voice.

"Who?" I asked unsure of who she was talking about.

"Sarah. I've read the book dad. You can't write emotion like that from something that only existed 20 plus years ago. You still feel that way don't you." I was not going to discuss my feelings with her about Sarah. There are things in life that your children do not need to know and to me this was one of them. She already knew, as did everyone else who knew me knows, I would always love Sarah.

"It's getting late. Goodnight Lindsey. I love you."

"Just tell me one thing first, if you ever had the chance again, what would you do differently?"

"Lindsey, there are so many choices I wish I had made differently. Pressuring her about time, the chick from Dundalk, letting her go and moving to the beach, gosh getting out of her car in the parking lot at the Community College, not showing up to the Ocean Club for dinner are just a few. I should have chased her down at Frostburg, I should have done everything I could have after not showing up at the beach, I should have stopped that wedding. I can't change those choices though. So many wrong choices where our lives could have been so different if we had just made the other choice, the choice to be with each other. Thinking about it breaks my heart." The thought of all the bad choices breaks my heart still to this day and I must constantly remind myself that life is the present, the future, and not the past.

She listened to every word I had to say. I believe she felt sorrow for my missed chances with Sarah. Maybe it was regret, I did not know but I could feel sadness in her that was meant for me.

"Did you ever find out why she was so sad at her Homecoming? Why she was a little withdrawn from a happy occasion like that? There must have been something seriously on her mind?"

Another question I was not sure how to answer so I decided to choose my words to where I could answer her but not betray the fact that I said I would never tell anyone as to why she was so distant that weekend. "I did Lindsey. That too breaks my heart. Our lives could have been so different because of that issue Sarah was dealing with, but in the end, there was nothing I could for her and that is all I will ever say about it."

A smile came across her face as if a happy thought had entered into her head "But now, what about now? If you had one more chance, what would you do now that you failed to do back then?" I did not hesitate in my answer.

"That's easy Lindsey." I smiled then said "I would love her. Simply love her."

"Goodnight Dad, I love you too." She said before hanging up the phone. I could tell she was smiling after hearing my answer remembering the song from Camelot and that line from it that Sarah had repeated to me so long ago.

58

    I spent the next day working on the second book. I was unaware of what time it was as I had no real windows in my basement apartment. I saw that my phone was blinking as if I had missed a call so needing the break, I decided to see who had called. I did not recognize the number, but I did realize it was a Maryland phone number from the area code of the number. I was curious now and I assumed it was a telemarketer. What the heck, I will call back. If I recognize the voice, I will say hello, if it is a telemarketer I can hang up. I dialed the number, and it was answered on the third ring.

    "Hi David. It's Sarah. I have been trying to reach you."

    To say I was shocked to hear her voice would be an understatement. I had to ask Sarah for clarification just to make sure and when she confirmed to me that it was indeed her, that it was my Sarah, I could not contain my excitement.

    We spent the next couple of hours catching up on life and by the time we were ready to hang up I had a huge grin on my face. Talking to Sarah was as easy as it was back in Highschool, or college, or anytime leading up to my not showing up to the Ocean Club, and somehow, I knew we would be talking again soon.

    "This is not goodbye David, but goodnight." She said to me before hanging up.

    Perfect I thought. Simply Perfect. I waited 25 years for it, but I finally had one more perfect moment with Sarah.

    Hope is so much more powerful than sorrow. The only thing stronger than hope is love. True love I mean. I passionately believe that people can fall in love with multiple people, but that "True Love" connection, that feeling you get when you know you are connected with this one person that can never be replaced, only happens with one person and it is something that should be treasured, built on, and cherished, no matter what the current situation in life is. It does not happen more than once so do not waste it if you find that with someone. Yes, true love conquers all if you allow it to. That is it. I have nothing more to say except maybe "I have no idea what the future will hold. All I know is that I have you right here, right now, and that's enough for me." And this time I would add "And I will forever love you."

The End

BOOKS BY THIS AUTHOR

Be Still, Enjoy The Silence

Prequel to The Endless Summers of Godbyes

Made in the USA
Middletown, DE
23 September 2023

39132573R00136